Hey!

Whose book is this?

Rosie
____

(write your name)

COOL!

Lincoln Peirce

BIG NATE
SUPER SCRIBBLER

BALZER + BRAY
An Imprint of HarperCollins*Publishers*

 For information address HarperCollins Children's Books, a division of HarperCollins Publishers, 195 Broadway, New York, NY 10007.
www.harpercollinschildrens.com
www.bignatebooks.com

Go to www.bignate.com to read the *Big Nate* comic strip.

ISBN 978-0-06-234922-4

Typography by Andrea Vandergrift
19 20 21 CG/LSCH 10 9 8 7 6 5 4 3
❖
First Edition

For Big Nate Fans Everywhere

Especially if you love…

scribble games,

messy lockers,

rockin' out,

hilarious comix,

egg salad (Okay, forget that last one.)

TEDDY SPECIALTY:
He does the best armpit fart in the whole sixth grade.

TRICKY TALENTS!

Teddy is one talented guy! List the 15 weirdest talents you know of.

1.
2.
3.
4. Ear wiggling
5.
6.
7. Crossing your eyes
8.
9.
10. Rolling your tongue
11.
12.
13.
14. Burping the alphabet
15.

JAZZ IT UP!

Dee Dee SERIOUSLY loves Jazzercise! Do you have dazzling dance moves? Draw lines from Column A to Column B to create brand-new dances.

Column A	Column B
FUNKY	FEET
HAPPY	POTATO
SILLY	CHICKEN
LOOSE	PINEAPPLE
RANDOM	GOOSE
HAIRY	BUNNY
MASHED	PEACOCK
SQUIRMY	ELASTIC
FUNNY	WORM
JAZZY	ELEPHANT

NOW WRITE DOWN ALL YOUR WILD NEW DANCE NAMES HERE!

1. Funky Feet
2. happy chicken
3. loose potato
4. random worm
5. funny goose
6. Jazzy Pineapple
7. hairy elephant
8. mashed peacock
9. silly elastick
10. mashed bunny

SHHHH!

Can you keep a secret? Use this alphabet to decode secret messages in this book. Become a super code cracker!

FIELD DAY FOLLIES

Hurray! It's Field Day at P.S. 38, and the sixth grade is ready to compete. Draw a line from each event to the correct picture below!

LONG JUMP

100-METER DASH

RELAY RACE

SOFTBALL THROW

1-MILE RUN

NOW SEE IF YOU CAN FIND ALL THE HIDDEN FIELD DAY GAMES IN THIS WORD PUZZLE!

TUG-OF-WAR

EGG TOSS

POTATO-SACK RACE

WHEELBARROW RACE

RELAY

WATER BALLOON TOSS

FRISBEE THROW

OBSTACLE COURSE

THREE-LEGGED RACE

W	B	G	E	A	L	S	W	G	O	S	O	I	O	E	B
O	O	A	G	C	R	T	H	R	C	T	D	C	C	L	E
R	N	E	O	E	T	H	H	H	Y	R	T	A	E	T	O
H	C	C	C	R	P	R	S	E	A	W	R	E	A	U	O
T	A	A	O	F	O	E	T	L	G	I	R	S	E	G	T
E	S	R	U	O	C	E	L	C	A	T	S	B	O	O	E
E	E	K	O	R	W	L	C	W	G	O	E	R	H	F	I
B	U	C	R	A	E	E	H	A	T	E	H	C	O	W	O
S	H	A	H	R	R	G	B	G	D	T	A	A	S	A	E
I	E	S	S	U	G	G	G	G	C	G	B	P	R	R	E
R	E	O	C	W	R	E	L	A	Y	S	R	A	W	A	E
F	R	T	T	L	E	D	O	E	T	C	S	S	R	S	A
E	C	A	R	W	O	R	R	A	B	L	E	E	H	W	B
W	A	T	E	R	B	A	L	L	O	O	N	T	O	S	S
A	G	O	O	R	O	C	L	R	I	E	E	R	T	S	O
R	W	P	C	E	W	E	S	R	E	T	A	L	R	T	S

FAMOUS FOOTWEAR

Nate makes his sneakers into a serious fashion statement. When he doodles on them, they become FABULOUS. Now you try!

DESIGN YOUR OWN ORIGINAL SNEAKERS HERE.

EXCLAMATION NATION

What is each character saying? You decide! Fill in the speech bubble and finish the scene.

bla bla bla bla bla
NATE DID YOU FALL ASLEEP!?
LARD
WE ARE ONLY HAVING DESERT
YAAAAAY!!
Bla Bla bla bla bla bla
SCIE

SCRIBBLE ME THIS!

Play the scribble game! It's time to turn this scribble into something SENSATIONAL. Then write a caption!

Your caption:

SNACK ATTACK

Chad and Nate are BIG fans of snacking. Nate LOVES Cheez Doodles, while Chad can't get enough sweets! Rate each snack from 1 (ho-hum) to 20 (wowza!). Then put a star by your top five.

FOOD	RANK
Pita chips	0/20
Oreos	10/20
Cheez Doodles	0/20
Brownies	5/20
Jerky	~~10~~ 17/20
Rice Krispy treats	4/20
Gingersnaps	1/20
Rice cakes	1/20
S'mores	20/20
Cabbage rolls	0/20
Cherries	10/20
Ice cream sandwich	20/20
Almonds	0/20
Chex Mix	5/20
Licorice	0/20
Celery sticks	0/20

SUPERHERO SENSATIONS

In Nate's comic "The Adventures of Ultra-Nate," Nate and his friends have secret superpowers. Fill in the speech bubbles and finish the scene!

WORD NERD

It's lunchtime! Using the letters in "cafetorium," see how many words you can create!

CAFETORIUM

1. cafe	11.
2. torium	12.
3. tori	13.
4. Afe	14.
5. caf	15.
6. Feto	16.
7. fet	17.
8. tore	18.
9.	19.
10.	20.

BREAKFAST BONANZA

Teddy loves having frozen waffles for breakfast, even if it sometimes gets him into sticky situations! What are <u>your</u> favorite breakfast foods? Find them in the word search on the opposite page.

PANCAKES
MUFFIN
SAUSAGE
OATMEAL
CREPES
BACON
DONUT
TOAST
COFFEE CAKE
GRAPEFRUIT
FROSTED FLAKES
POP TART
SCRAMBLED EGGS
HASH BROWNS
BREAKFAST SANDWICH

A	I	D	P	C	M	T	T	G	F	T	I	R	C	F	E	E
S	C	F	O	C	A	F	W	A	E	R	G	S	A	A	F	O
H	C	I	W	D	N	A	S	T	S	A	F	K	A	E	R	B
T	G	R	O	D	O	A	A	N	F	T	R	E	M	R	O	A
K	E	B	A	O	C	A	U	O	W	P	E	E	A	T	S	R
O	O	C	H	M	A	R	S	S	R	O	O	G	T	R	T	N
C	T	F	U	W	B	P	A	I	C	P	R	N	C	S	E	N
P	R	S	F	H	C	L	G	R	O	A	A	B	G	P	D	G
E	A	S	N	A	O	R	E	S	F	G	C	E	H	O	F	E
D	U	T	A	C	B	P	E	D	F	E	D	G	N	S	L	L
O	T	S	A	S	G	R	A	P	E	F	R	U	I	T	A	F
R	A	L	M	U	F	F	I	N	E	G	T	R	R	M	K	H
W	H	D	O	H	M	L	A	H	C	S	G	C	W	G	E	O
L	A	B	A	E	T	E	E	W	A	A	T	S	T	A	S	B
S	S	E	K	E	T	S	N	O	K	E	K	R	L	B	O	E
O	A	A	U	W	S	A	T	R	E	L	A	E	M	T	A	O
E	L	M	E	H	F	P	E	E	T	L	F	O	S	M	E	C

READY? SET. POP QUIZ!

Are you a MEGA Big Nate fan? Test your Nate know-how and take his quiz!

1. Nate can make a basket from mid-court, backwards, with his eyes closed.

☐ TRUE ☐ FALSE

2. Nate likes to bonk himself on the head with a plastic bottle.

☐ TRUE ☐ FALSE

3. Nate's good luck charm is a plastic lizard.

☐ TRUE ☐ FALSE

4. Nate's superhero name is Notorious Nate!

☐ TRUE ☑ FALSE

5. Nate plays beanbag Olympics in the library.

☑ TRUE ☐ FALSE

6. Nate's sister has a boyfriend.

☑ TRUE ☐ FALSE

7. Nate once had Eskimo Day–themed lunch at school.

☐ TRUE ☑ FALSE

8. Nate's band's name is Kill the Clam.

☐ TRUE ☑ FALSE

MUSIC MAN

Nate's band, Enslave the Mollusk, has been invited to play at the school assembly! Unscramble the words below to uncover each instrument.

RUDM D r u m

GTUARI G u t a i r

NETOMRBO _ _ _ _ _ _ _ _

BOOE _ _ _ _

TEFLU _ _ _ _ _

ABSS _ _ _ _

____

PLAY ALONG!

Join the official ENSLAVE THE MOLLUSK fan club!

KNOCK, KNOCK!

Nate's teacher Mr. Staples has a knack for knock-knock jokes. Using the secret code below, figure out the punch lines.

A	B	C	D	E	F	G	H	I	J	K	L	M
Z	Y	X	W	V	U	T	S	R	Q	P	O	N

N	O	P	Q	R	S	T	U	V	W	X	Y	Z
M	L	K	J	I	H	G	F	E	D	C	B	A

Q: Knock, knock.
Who's there?
Who.
Who who?

A: R H   G S V I V

Z M   L D O   R M

S V I V ?

Q: Knock, knock.
Who's there?
Leaf.
Leaf who?

A: _ _ _ _   _ _   _ _ _ _ _.
O V Z U   N V   Z O L M V

Q: Knock, knock.
Who's there?
Lettuce.
Lettuce who?

A: _ _ _ _ _ _ _   _ _,
O V G G F X V   R M,

_ _ _   _ _ _   _ _
Z M W   B L F   O O

_ _ _ _   _ _ _.
U R M W   L F G

COMIX DRAMA!

Whoa! What happens when Mega-Chad takes on Mrs. Godzilla? Draw it!

+

= ?

YOUR TITLE HERE

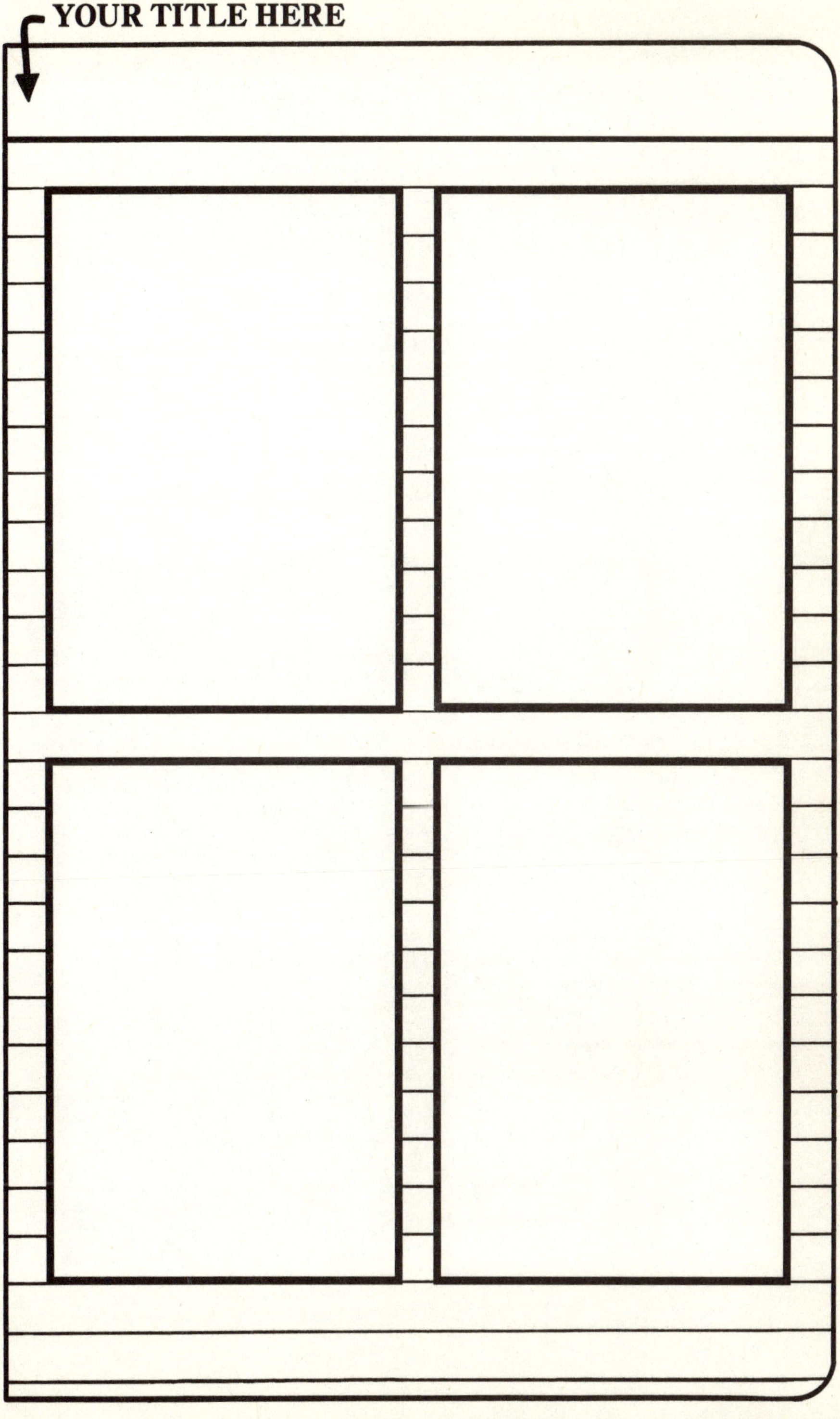

DRAMATIC FLASHBACK!

It's time to <u>rewind</u>! In the boxes below, draw what happened moments before each scene.

SCRIBBLE SPRINT!

On your mark, get set, GO! Play the scribble game, SUPERFAST! Time yourself to see how speedy you can be.

Now create one very cool caption!

Write your time! :

HERO HOUR

Nate is a master at drawing superheroes. He created a brand-new hero based on his buddy called: MEGA-CHAD!

FILL IN THE BLANKS TO CREATE NEW SUPERHERO NAMES FOR EACH CHARACTER.

Gina the ______________

______________ Nate!

Godfrey ______________

______________ Francis

Teddy the ______________

______________ Dee Dee

Ellen ______________

______________ Artur

Randy the ______________

______________ Jenny!

WHAT WOULD <u>YOUR</u> SUPERHERO NAME BE?

AWESOME!

NOW DRAW YOUR SUPERHERO COSTUME.

IT'S TIME TO FIGHT CRIME!

COPY THAT!

Are you a clever cartoonist like Nate? Copy each character in a blank box below.

GO!
GO!

MIDDLE SCHOOL MASH-UP

Unscramble the names below, then draw a line from each name to the correct kid!

YAAM _ _ _ _

CRMAUS _ _ _ _ _ _

DCHA _ _ _ _

ANET _ _ _ _

YEDDT _ _ _ _ _

NEJNY _ _ _ _ _

RATRU _ _ _ _ _

EEDDEE _ _ _ _ _ _

SIBLING RIVALRY

Nate and his sister, Ellen, don't always get along. But sometimes that leads to Nate's brightest ideas! Fill in the bubbles and decide on Nate's discovery!

COMIX R US

It's cartooning time! What happens when Principal Nichols catches Nate and Chad in the hall with a beanbag? Trouble!

+

= ?

CREATE YOUR COMIC HERE.

NO EXCUSES!

Have you ever given your teacher crazy excuses for not turning in your homework? Nate sure has. But Mrs. Godfrey (aka Godzilla) won't let him get away with it!

LIST YOUR TOP 15 WILDEST EXCUSES EVER.

1.

2. The cat ate it, then threw it up!

3.

4.

5.

6.

7. The mailman accidentally took it!

8.

9.

10.

11.

12.

13. My baby sister flushed it down the toilet.

14.

15.

DREAM ON!

Nate, Francis, Teddy, and Artur are in a band called Enslave the Mollusk. Fill in the bubbles below and decide what would happen at one of their gigs!

ARE YOU IN A BAND? WHAT WOULD YOU TITLE YOUR SONGS? LIST ALL YOUR IDEAS HERE!

1.
2.
3.
4.
5.
6. Rock On, Rock Off
7.
8.
9.
10. School Day Blues
11.
12.
13.
14.
15.

LUCKY LOCKER

If you filled your locker with all your favorite things, what would they be?

LIST YOUR TOP 20!

1.
2.
3.
4.
5.
6.
7.
8.
9.
10.

11.

12.

13.

14.

15.

16.

17.

18.

19.

20.

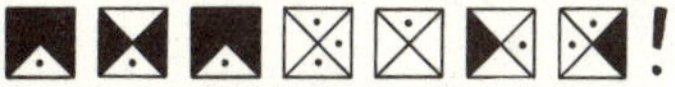

MESSY MAZE!

Nate's locker is a TOTAL mess.
Can you help him find his way through it?

DOODLE-LICIOUS

Are you an awesome artist? Do you dare to doodle day and night like Nate? Then go crazy and fill the page!

CHILLAX

Nate has a special habit that helps him relax—he bonks himself on the head with a plastic bottle! What do you do to relax? Put down your TOP 15—bonus points for more!

1.

2. Eat marshmallows

3.

4.

5. Watch a movie

6.

7.

8.

9.

10.

11. Play with my hamster

12.

13.

14.

15.

FITNESS ZONE

P.S. 38 has been declared a Fitness Zone! Are you ready to sweat it out? See if you can find all these sports in the puzzle on the opposite page!

WRESTLING

SOCCER

BASKETBALL

GYMNASTICS

SOFTBALL

SAILING

AEROBICS

SWIMMING

VOLLEYBALL

LACROSSE

HOCKEY

TRACK

B	V	A	E	K	R	T	A	I	S	O	A
K	O	G	S	A	A	R	S	B	O	L	K
C	L	L	A	B	T	E	K	S	A	B	I
A	L	A	W	N	V	S	O	C	M	I	S
R	E	C	C	O	S	F	R	I	A	A	A
T	Y	O	R	O	T	O	Y	T	E	Y	I
R	B	L	B	B	S	K	N	S	R	B	L
C	A	I	A	S	L	C	E	A	O	L	I
I	L	L	E	S	C	Y	I	N	B	O	N
C	L	C	Y	S	W	I	M	M	I	N	G
C	R	B	H	O	C	K	E	Y	C	S	S
W	R	E	S	T	L	I	N	G	S	S	T

FRANTIC ROMANTIC

Poor Nate just can't seem to get a date! Draw lines from Column A to Column B to decide who makes the cutest couples.

FREAK-OUT!

Watch out—Nate's scariest teacher, Mrs. Godfrey, is having a total meltdown. Fill in the speech bubbles and decide Nate's fate!

JACKPOT!

Teddy's thinking BIG—he wants to win the lottery or be elected president someday! What would YOUR jackpots be? List them here, then rank them from 1 to 10!

JACKPOT MOMENT	RANK
1.	
2.	
3. Going into space	
4.	
5.	

6. ______

7. ______

8. ______

9. ______

10. ______

11. ______

12. Having my own TV show ______

13. ______

14. ______

15. ______

DRAW-A-THON

Pick up that pencil and put your skills to the test. Copy each drawing in one of the blank boxes below.

CAPTION ATTRACTION

Yikes! Something crazy is happening in these scenes. Write a caption for each!

UH..
HNK!

OOLP!
CJ

☆ ☆ ☆ P. S. 38'S ☆ ☆ ☆ "LEAST LIKELY TO GET ☆ DETENTION" CLUB! ☆

Here's one club Nate will NEVER belong to: the "Least Likely to Get Detention Club"! Draw lines from each name to the correct kid!

GINA HEMPHILL-TOMS
Yes, she **DID** get detention once (thank you, Ben Franklin).

NOELLE NICHOLS
She's the principal's niece, so even if she does something wrong, she's teflon.

BRAD MACKLIN
... because he's just too much of a wuss wagon to ever get in trouble.

KAREN McFADDEN
She's in the Peer Counseling Society, so she knows all about avoiding conflict.

ARTUR PASHKOV
It's impossible to get detention when you're **PERFECT IN EVERY WAY.**

PAJAMA PARTY

Check out Nate's cool pajamas—do you have Pajama Day at your school? Draw the pj's you would wear!

ANNOYING ARTUR

Why must Artur be <u>SO</u> incredibly perfect all the time? It drives Nate nuts! Fill in the speech bubbles and figure out what Artur's done now.

DOODLEY DOO

Take a break, grab your pen, and set your brain free! Doodle all over this page!

COMIX CRUSADER

Comic relief to the rescue! What happens when a rock star meets Dee Dee with Chad's lucky foot? Can you say "drama"? Draw it!

+

+

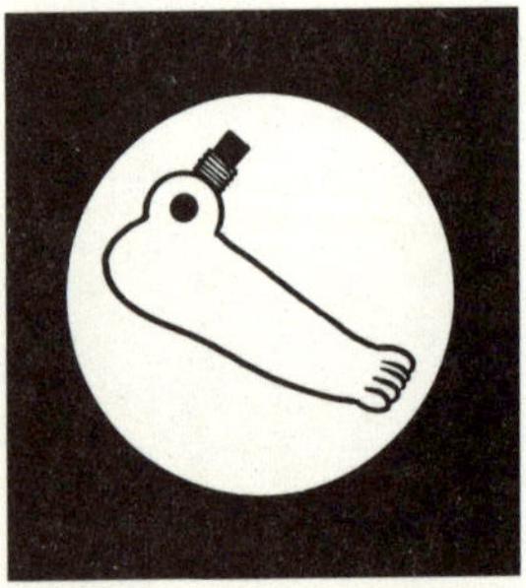

=

?

YOUR TITLE HERE

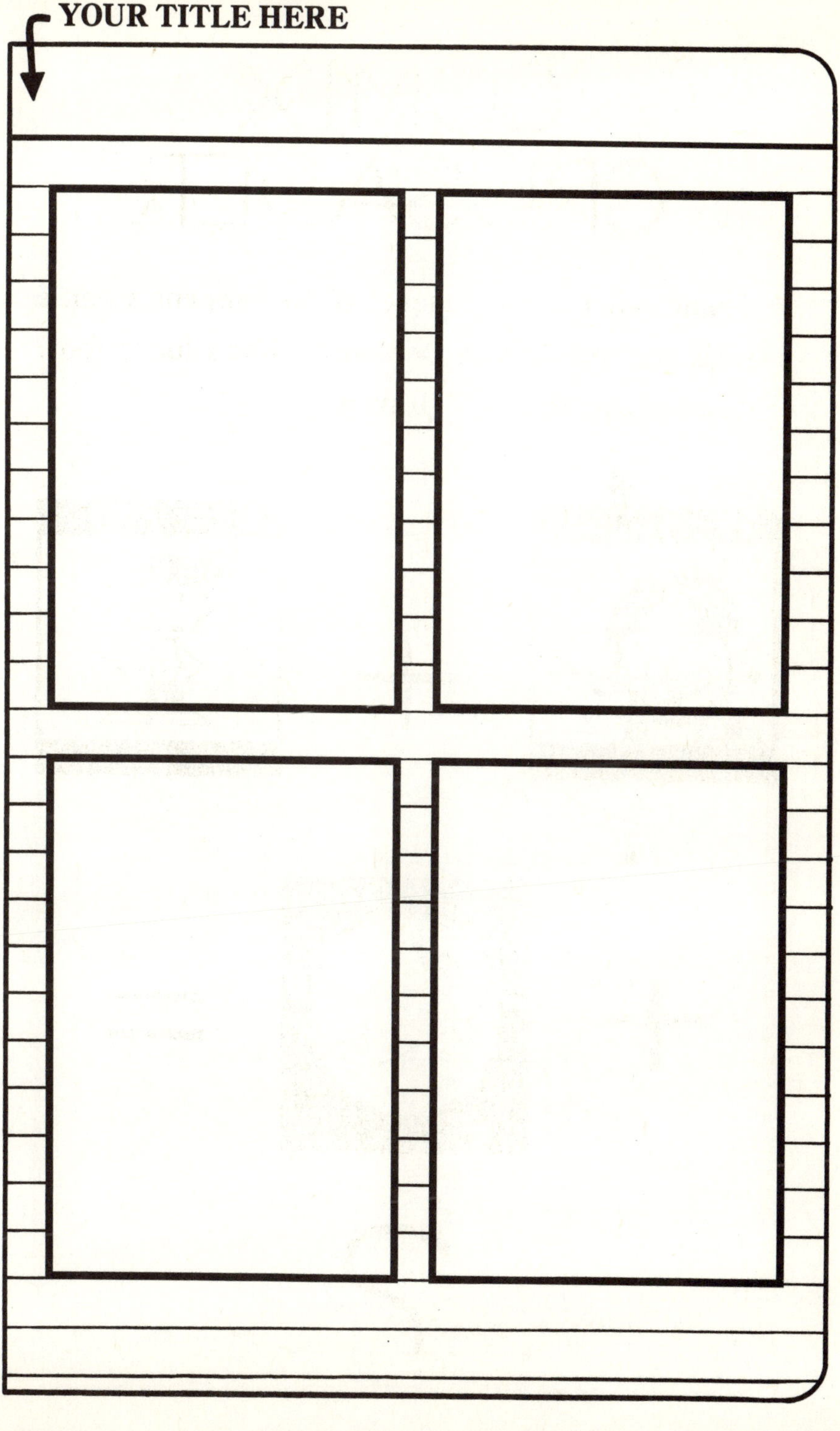

ROLL CALL

How well
do you know
Nate's crew?
Solve the puzzle
and see if you
can guess
who's who!

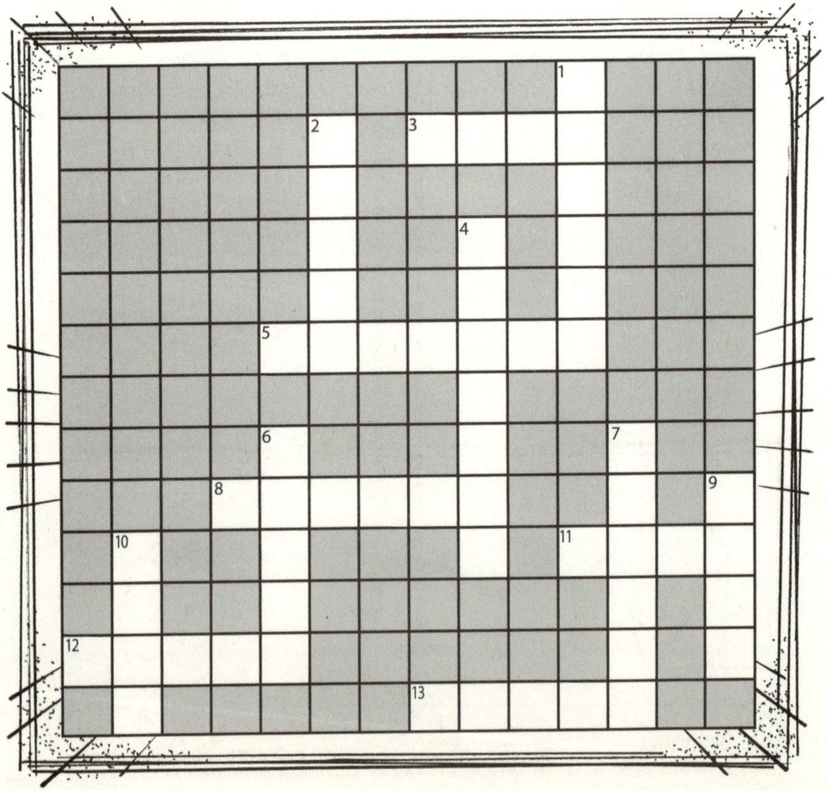

CLUES

ACROSS

3. Chad is in love with her.

5. The master of trivia—Nate's #1 best friend.

8. She's got LOTS of drama.

11. Only gets straight A's. The teacher's pet!

12. The original bully.

13. One very funny dude—Nate's OTHER best friend.

DOWN

1. The meanest seventh grader at P.S. 38.

2. Annoyingly perfect.

4. In love with Spitsy.

6. Nate's crush, who's dating Artur!

7. Likes to drool. Eats his own poop.

9. Just call him Mr. Awesome.

10. Nate's sidekick—he may be small, but he's got super spirit!

BACK TO THE FUTURE

Can you predict the future? Look into your crystal ball and draw what happens next.

I GUARANTEE IT!

Boys, I represent a MAJOR record label! I'm offering you a CONTRACT!
WOW!

BOBCATS

THREE-LEGGED RACE

Coach loves the three-legged race. Draw lines from Column A to Column B to create the funniest teams ever!

Column A	Column B
SPITSY	GINA
MRS. HICKSON	MAYA
RANDY	JENNY
NICK BLONSKY	NATE'S DAD
ELLEN	CHAD
MARCUS	FRANCIS
MRS. GODFREY	TEDDY
PRINCIPAL NICHOLS	MS. BRINDLE
COACH JOHN	PICKLES
NATE	MR. ROSA

CHOOSE THE MOST HILARIOUS PARTNERS AND DRAW THEM HERE!

ROCK 'N' ROLL

Nate's band is ready to rock, and the crowd is going wild! Fill in the speech bubbles and let the show begin!

WHO'S YOUR FAVORITE ROCK STAR?

SKETCH A PICTURE HERE.

ARE YOU A SERIOUS GROUPIE?

LIST THE BANDS YOU CAN'T LIVE WITHOUT!

1.
2.
3.
4.
5.
6.
7.
8.
9.
10.
11.
12.
13.
14.
15.

FLOWER POWER

Solve the maze (by new kid Breckenridge Puffington III). He LOVES drawing flowers.

SCRIBBLE SLAM

Let's take it up a notch! Turn this scribble into the strangest animal you can image!

Now come up with three different names for it!

1.
2.
3.

Put a star by your favorite!

GROSS ME OUT!

Are there some things you find SICKENING? Like Nate's least favorite food, egg salad? Or couples that slobber all over each other?

NAME THE TOP 25 THINGS THAT GROSS YOU OUT.

1.
2.
3.
4. banana slugs
5.
6.
7.
8. soy crackers
9.
10.
11.
12.
13. creepy clowns
14.
15.
16.
17. cat vomit
18.
19.
20.
21.
22. moldy cheese
23.
24.
25.

SMARTY-PANTS

The clock is ticking. . . .

Test your Big Nate knowledge NOW!

1. Mrs. Hickson works in the cafetorium.

☐ TRUE ☐ FALSE

2. Maya is a seventh grader.

☐ TRUE ☐ FALSE

3. Chad's good luck charm is a four-leaf clover.

☐ TRUE ☐ FALSE

4. Marcus thinks he's Mr. Cool.

☐ TRUE ☐ FALSE

5. Nate did really well on his report card.

☐ TRUE ☐ FALSE

6. Nate likes to bonk his head with a basketball.

☐ TRUE ☐ FALSE

7. Chad has a huge crush on Maya.

☐ TRUE ☐ FALSE

8. Randy is a fan of Jazzercise.

☐ TRUE ☐ FALSE

9. Nate once got gum on his butt.

☐ TRUE ☐ FALSE

10. Nate forgets all the words to his song at assembly.

☐ TRUE ☐ FALSE

**BONUS:

Chad LOVES wasabi peas.

☐ TRUE ☐ FALSE

HOCKEY TALK

Nate, Chad, and their friends play hockey in gym class—can you find all these hockey terms in the puzzle on the opposite page?

GOAL

PUCK

STICK

DRILL

PASS

PLAYER

DEFENSE

CREASE

PENALTY SHOT

FACE-OFF

RED LIGHT

PRACTICE

C	E	F	A	C	E	O	F	F	L	E	L	B	I
L	D	D	C	N	C	T	A	L	K	I	L	K	I
L	R	B	E	A	I	C	E	I	E	R	F	C	A
D	I	N	L	D	T	F	R	S	B	R	I	I	K
E	L	D	R	I	C	R	E	A	S	E	R	T	S
F	L	W	S	E	A	E	D	Y	I	L	L	S	L
E	E	R	P	I	R	P	L	I	O	R	A	N	A
N	C	O	N	N	P	P	I	R	W	P	L	C	D
S	A	L	B	L	L	Y	G	N	A	P	D	R	A
E	S	Z	A	L	E	R	H	R	B	U	O	L	L
N	F	Y	M	O	I	O	T	W	L	C	I	R	D
L	E	L	L	S	G	R	L	E	D	K	O	L	N
R	P	E	N	A	L	T	Y	S	H	O	T	S	B
L	C	C	R	O	B	L	A	E	L	I	R	C	S

GOOD DAY, SUNSHINE

Nate's luck sure is changing—he's having one AWESOME week! Fill in the speech bubbles and write captions for each day below.

MARCUS MADNESS

Boy, Marcus sure is mean and grumpy! Copy the many faces of Marcus in the blank boxes and put him in his place!

SHOVE!

GOOD GODFREY!

How well do you know Mrs. Godfrey, Nate's nemesis?

1. Nate has many nicknames for Mrs. Godfrey, but his favorite is . . .

   a. Great Hairball
   b. Godzilla
   c. Ingrown Toenail
   d. Swamp Monster

2. Mrs. Godfrey teaches which class?

   a. Math
   b. English
   c. Gym
   d. Social studies

3. Who is Mrs. Godfrey's favorite student?

a. Jenny

b. Francis

c. Gina

d. Artur

4. If Mrs. Godfrey looked in Nate's desk, what WOULDN'T she find?

a. Cheez Doodles

b. Neat notes

c. Comix

d. An empty plastic bottle

5. Choose the thing that Mrs. Godfrey DOES NOT do.

a. Desk inspections

b. Give A's

c. Dance the macarena

d. Surprise her students with pop quizzes

LITTLE-KID LINEUP

Look at Dee Dee when she was little—she's SO cute! Now draw each character below as a little kid, too!

CHAD

NATE

FRANCIS

TEDDY

JENNY

NOW EVERYONE WANTS TO KNOW. . . .

WHAT DID <u>YOU</u> LOOK LIKE AS A LITTLE KID?

DRAW YOUR MINI-ME HERE!

DANCE, DEE DEE!

Dee Dee's one dazzling dancer—using the letters in the words "dancing shoes," see how many other words you can make!

DANCING SHOES

1.
2.
3.
4.
5.
6.
7.
8.
9.
10.
11.
12.
13.
14.
15.
16.
17.
18.
19.
20.

CRAZY COMIX!

There's serious suspense here! What happens when Dad and Coach are faced with Nate on his drums? Draw a comic of this drum drama!

+

+

=

?

YOUR TITLE HERE

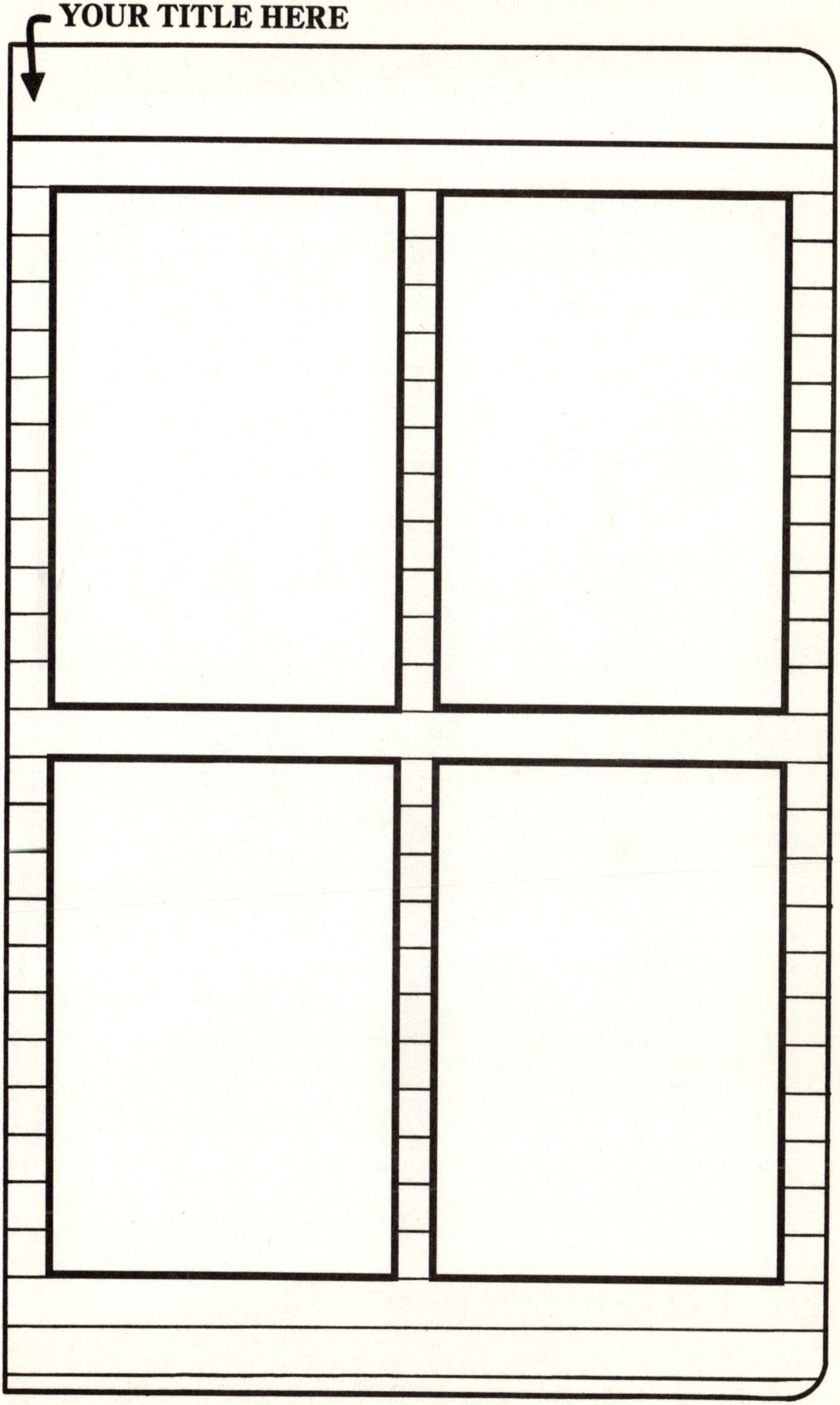

ALWAYS-PERFECT ARTUR

Nate is tired of being outdone by Artur, aka Mr. Perfect. Draw lines from Column A to Column B and come up with Nate's many nicknames for him!

Column A	Column B
Fart	-o-matic
Pea	Boy
Wussy	Brain
Zit	Monkey
Weasel	Toenail
Glass of	Dry Toast
Slug	Bucket
Ingrown	Prune Juice
Booger	Wagon
Piece of	Cuddle
Sweat	Bunny
Barf	Kins

WRITE YOUR ZANY NEW NICKNAMES FOR ARTUR HERE!

1. ______________________________

2. ______________________________

3. ______________________________

4. ______________________________

5. ______________________________

6. ______________________________

7. ______________________________

8. ______________________________

9. ______________________________

10. ______________________________

11. ______________________________

12. ______________________________

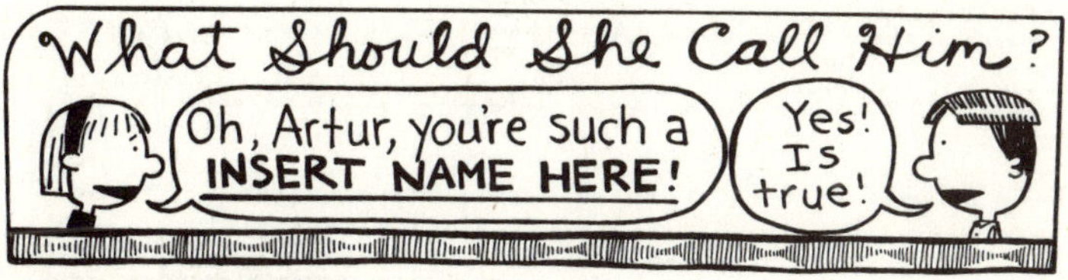

SCRIBBLE DRIBBLE

See if you can turn this scribble into something terrific before Nate has time to make a basket!

Now name it!

NATURE FREAK

New kid Breckenridge LOVES plants. Draw your favorite tree, bush, or plant here.

DESK INSPECTION!

Watch out! Super strict Mrs. Godfrey is doing a desk inspection. What would she find in your desk?

LIST ALL THE ITEMS HERE!

1.

2.

3.

4.

5.

6.

7.

8.

9.

10.

11.

12.

13.

14.

15.

I DREAM OF GINA!

Nate's archenemy, Gina, LOVES to be the teacher's pet! Next to each scene below, write what Gina would say.

GINA SAYS:

____

____

____

GINA SAYS:

____

____

____

GINA SAYS:

____

____

____

GINA SAYS:

GINA SAYS:

GINA SAYS:

GINA SAYS:

GOOD NIGHT, NATE!

Before Nate heads to bed, he puts on his comfy pajamas, brushes his teeth, and draws comix. What's your bedtime ritual?

WRITE IT HERE:

1.

2.

3.

4.

5.

6.

7.

8.

9.

10.

11.

12.

13.

14.

15.

DOODLE CANOODLE

Quick! Doodle away

and draw everything you <u>LOVE</u> on this page!

STORY SWAP

It's Breakfast Book Club! Sounds yummy, right?
Match each kid to the title of the book they're reading.

A DAY IN THE LIFE OF MRS. GODFREY

Gah! Try filling the shoes of Nate's most hated teacher! Describe the daily life of crazy Mrs. Godfrey in the bubbles below.

Soon...
FOOM!
LATER, IN THE FACULTY LOUNGE...
HOT TUB
END!

NEW-KID NO-NO'S

Nate has to show the new kid around school. Do you have some expert advice, too? Tell him what not to do.

LIST YOUR TOP 20 NEW-KID NO-NO'S:

1.

2.

3.

4. Don't bring a stinky lunch!

5.

6.

7.

8.

9. Leave the little-kid backpack at home. Find one with style.

10.

11.

12.

13. Don't wipe your nose on your sleeve!

14.

15.

16.

17.

18.

19.

20.

CARRIED AWAY!

Where is Nate headed? Set your inner artist free and decorate all the balloons on the opposite page!

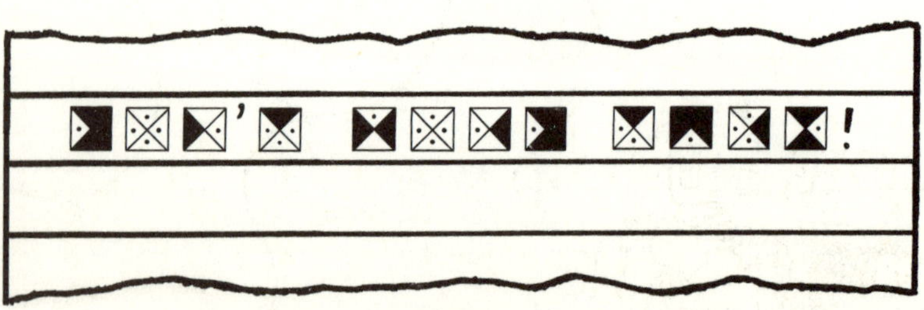

THE SKY'S THE LIMIT

Can Nate and his friends get to the top?

SCRIBBLICIOUS

Do you get hungry for an empty page? Well, this is one serious scribble snack. Turn this scribble into your favorite food!

TOUCHDOWN!

When Principal Nichols gives the gang a surprise recess, Nate's game to play football with Roderick and his crew. Find all these words in the puzzle and win big!

DEFENSE

FIELD GOAL

TOUCHDOWN

QUARTERBACK

TACKLE

PASS

KICK

BLOCK

PLAY

K	H	T	O	U	C	H	D	O	W	N
U	C	M	N	E	L	K	C	A	T	P
L	M	A	M	B	B	C	M	P	H	L
A	Y	K	B	B	Z	O	L	W	C	A
O	D	I	C	R	D	L	R	C	X	Y
G	N	E	P	I	E	B	C	B	U	S
D	T	K	F	A	K	T	U	L	P	M
L	G	S	E	E	S	Z	R	C	C	K
E	C	X	F	J	N	S	B	A	X	C
I	B	S	M	G	J	S	J	W	U	Z
F	G	D	R	Y	A	M	E	J	U	Q

CUTE METER

Chad just found out that Maya thinks he's ADORABLE! Wow. Rank these things on the cute meter from "Aww" to "Adorable"!

1. Pickles the cat (aka Spitsy's crush)

☐ AWW ☐ SUPER CUTE
☐ SWEET ☐ ADORABLE

2. A big basket of puppies

☐ AWW ☐ SUPER CUTE
☐ SWEET ☐ ADORABLE

3. Baby panda bear

☐ AWW ☐ SUPER CUTE
☐ SWEET ☐ ADORABLE

4. A sea otter swimming on its back

☐ AWW ☐ SUPER CUTE
☐ SWEET ☐ ADORABLE

5. Mini cupcakes

- ☐ AWW
- ☐ SWEET
- ☐ SUPER CUTE
- ☐ ADORABLE

6. A hedgehog

- ☐ AWW
- ☐ SWEET
- ☐ SUPER CUTE
- ☐ ADORABLE

7. A kitten in a teacup

- ☐ AWW
- ☐ SWEET
- ☐ SUPER CUTE
- ☐ ADORABLE

8. Parade of penguins, wearing pants

- ☐ AWW
- ☐ SWEET
- ☐ SUPER CUTE
- ☐ ADORABLE

9. Your latest selfie*

- ☐ AWW
- ☐ SWEET
- ☐ SUPER CUTE
- ☐ ADORABLE

*DRAW ONE HERE.

BANDMATES

Can you fill in the grid so that each band member only appears once in every row, column, and box?

F = **FRANCIS**

T = **TEDDY**

N = **NATE**

A = **ARTUR**

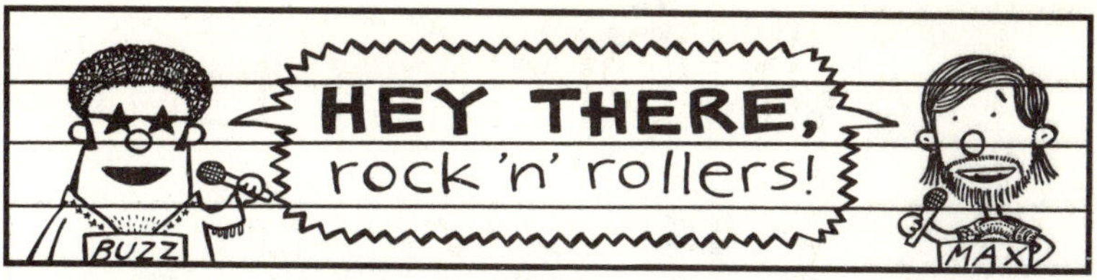
HEY THERE,
rock 'n' rollers!
BUZZ
MAX

N			T
			A
F			

SQUEEEAALL!
OMG! I LOVE this song!

TEAM TRIUMPH

Chad and Maya were the winning team in the three-legged race on Field Day! Why? Because they worked together! Grab a friend and see how many words you can create using the letters in "teamwork."

TEAMWORK

1.	11.
2.	12. wok
3.	13.
4.	14.
5. tame	15.
6.	16.
7.	17.
8.	18.
9.	19.
10.	20.

NOW DRAW YOUR OWN FIELD DAY TEAM BELOW!

TEAM NAME:

TEAM CAPTAIN:

TEAM COLOR:

DRAWING DEAD ZONE!

Here are the things Nate hates to draw. Let's see if you can do better than Nate! Draw your own version in each blank box below.

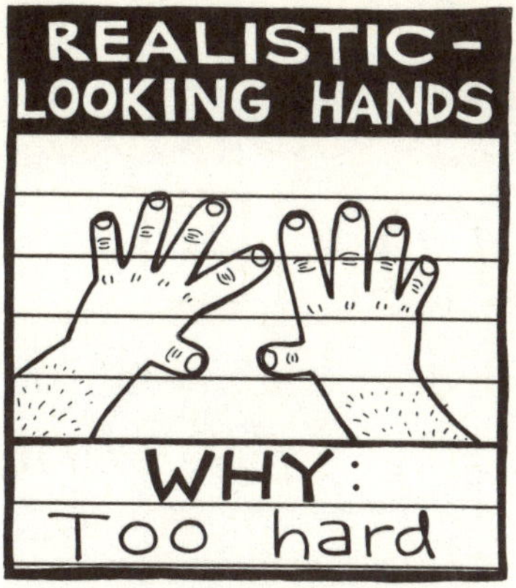

DRAW THE MEANEST BULLY YOU KNOW.

LONG, LONG AGO

Mrs. Hickson reads to Nate's class from a journal that was written one hundred years ago! What was your town like then? Just imagine! Check out Ms. Clarke's lesson, then turn the page to fill in the blanks.

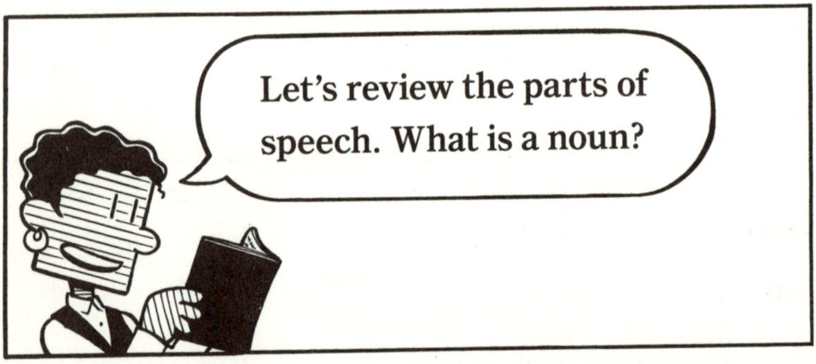

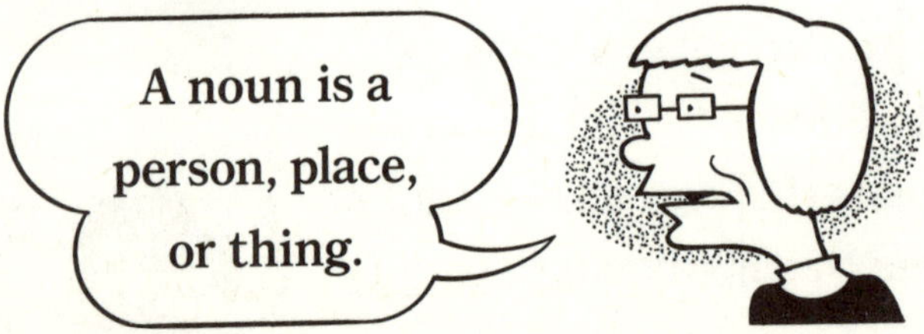

EXAMPLES:

Principal Nichols (person), school (place), homework (thing)

EXAMPLES: write, play, sleep

EXAMPLES:
funny (Teddy's jokes)
snarky (Gina's comebacks)
smart (Francis!)

MAKE A LIST OF THE SILLIEST WORDS YOU CAN THINK OF:

1. Adjective:
2. Noun:
3. Noun:
4. Noun:
5. Noun:
6. Noun:
7. Adjective:
8. Noun:
9. Noun:
10. Adjective:
11. Noun:
12. Noun:
13. Adjective:
14. Noun:
15. Noun:
16. Verb:
17. Verb:
18. Adjective:
19. Noun:

NOW FILL IN THE BLANKS
TO TELL YOUR STORY!

One hundred years ago, my town had ______________ (1.)

people living there, and most of its citizens worked

as ______________ (2.), ______________ (3.), or ______________ (4.).

For fun they would go downtown and play

______________ (5.) or ______________ (6.).

They wore ______________ (7.) ______________ (8.) when

they dressed up for a special occasion, and their

favorite sport was ____________ (9.), because the weather was ____________ (10.). They didn't have ____________ (11.) or ____________ (12.), which is ____________ (13.)!

Everyone ate ____________ (14.) for breakfast and ____________ (15.) for dinner. I would ____________ (16.) if I had to eat that! Luckily, I ____________ (17.) in the ____________ (18.) ____________ (19.)!

CESSPOOL'S CRISIS

There's some seriously weird surgery going on here—fill in the speech bubbles and finish the story!

ROYAL HIGHNESS

Nate's in charge of being a buddy to the new kid, Breckenridge Puffington III. Sounds like a prince's name, right? What would your royal life look like?

YOU DECIDE!

ROYAL NAME

____

____

YOUR CROWN

YOUR ROYAL OUTFIT

YOUR SCEPTER
(of course!)

YOUR QUEEN OR KING
(Who's your crush?)

THE MAGICAL LAND
YOU RULE OVER!

ADVENTURES OF BUDDY BOY

The new kid already has his very own superhero persona: Buddy Boy! Will he help Ultra-Nate fight crime? You decide.

NURSE'S OFFICE

Nate's just a little bit used to accidents. And this time he has to visit the nurse, Mrs. Albert! Find all the words related to the nurse's office in the word scramble and help him get better, fast!

STETHOSCOPE
SCRAPE
RUNNY NOSE
SCRUBS
THERMOMETER
MEDICINE
BANDAGE
LOLLIPOP
COUGH SYRUP
CLIPBOARD
SORE THROAT
FEVER

E	R	H	P	O	P	I	L	L	O	L	E	E
C	T	S	P	N	V	O	C	U	C	S	T	O
S	E	I	P	P	O	F	N	T	C	U	S	R
S	T	A	O	R	H	T	E	R	O	S	E	O
T	O	E	H	E	O	R	U	V	G	O	H	B
S	O	B	T	T	P	B	C	P	E	U	E	A
C	O	U	G	H	S	Y	R	U	P	R	N	N
R	E	T	E	M	O	M	R	E	H	T	I	D
A	U	V	L	U	O	S	N	E	T	O	C	A
P	D	S	E	H	S	H	C	M	O	O	I	G
E	E	E	C	L	I	P	B	O	A	R	D	E
C	A	I	O	T	R	N	E	E	P	S	E	A
T	H	R	U	N	N	Y	N	O	S	E	M	A

COMIX TRIX!

What happens when Nick Blonsky meets Principal Nichols AND lovebirds Artur and Jenny? U DRAW IT!

+

+

=

?

YOUR TITLE HERE

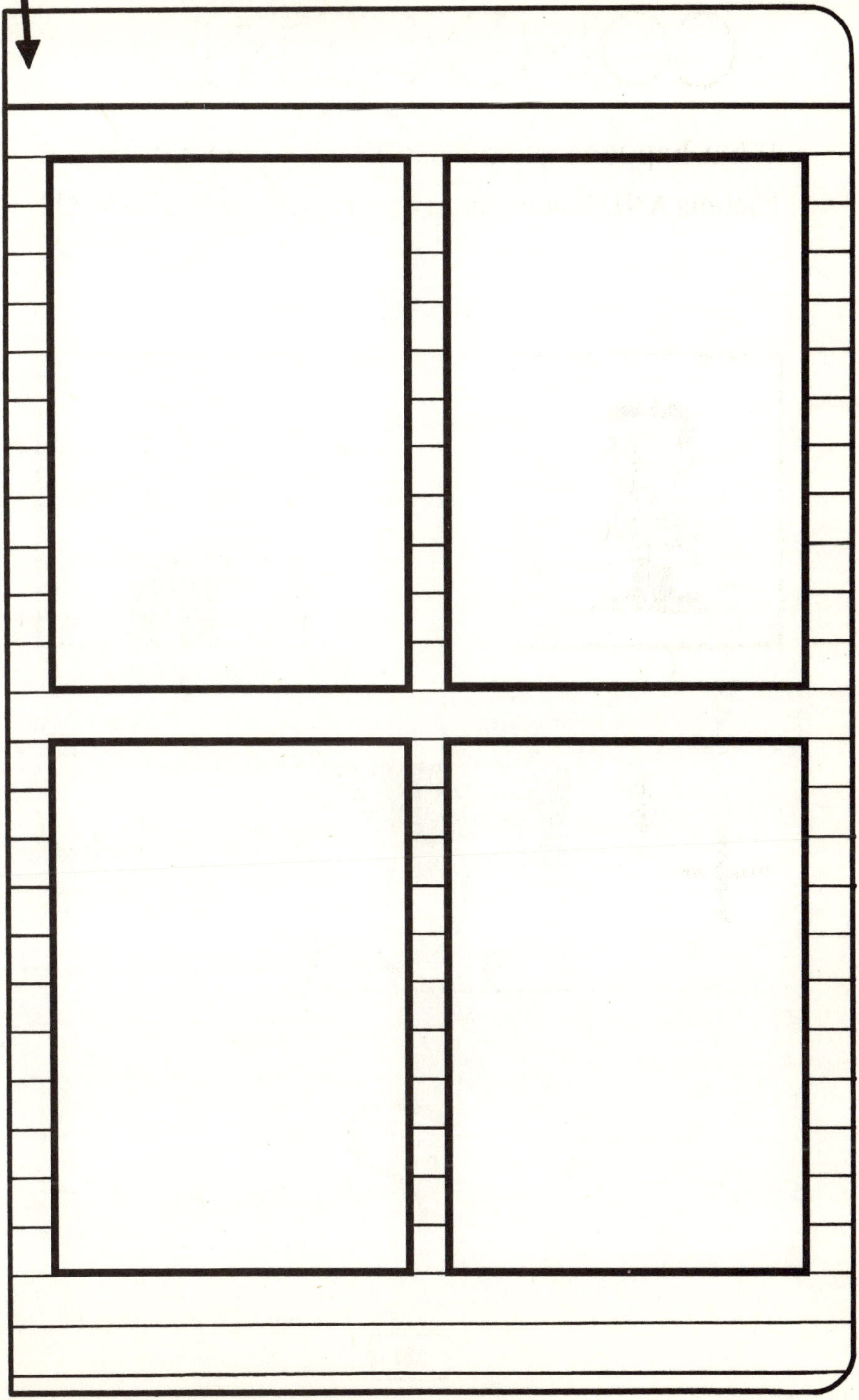

CAPTION REACTION

Wow! Nate found photos of P.S. 38's most memorable moments—write a caption for each picture!

MAKE 'EM SWEAT!

Coach John is one tough gym teacher! List your <u>TOP 15</u> gym class activities that really make you sweat. Star the toughest ones!

1.
2.
3.
4.
5.
6.
7.
8.
9.
10.
11.
12.
13.
14.
15.

Now come up with adjectives for each letter of Coach John's name. Quick, before he gives you another push-up!

C ____________________

O ____________________

A ____________________

C ranky ____________________

H ____________________

J ____________________

O ____________________

H ____________________

N ____________________

ART CLASS ANTICS

Nate's favorite class is art with Mr. Rosa! Rank all your classes from 1 (ho-hum) to 10 (terrific!) below. Put a star by your favorite!

SCIENCE ________

MATH ________

GYM ________

ENGLISH ________

SOCIAL STUDIES ________

MUSIC ________

ART ________

NOW DRAW THE CRAZIEST ART PROJECT YOU CAN THINK OF!

SCRIBBLE SLAM!

Get your pencils ready! Finish this scribble faster than Chad can eat a jelly donut. GO!

Now name your creation!

COMIX R US!

It's time to design! Dazzle Nate and his friends. Create one super cool comic book cover here that might even impress Gina.

TITLE: ______________________________

AUTHOR: ______________________________

STARRING: ______________________________
(superhero)

LAUGH ATTACK

Don't let Randy have the last laugh! Use Teddy's secret code from page 22 to figure out the punch lines to these jokes!

Q: Why are ghosts bad liars?

A: _ _ _ _ _ _ _   _ _ _
Y V X Z F H V   B L F

_ _ _   _ _ _   _ _ _ _ _
X Z M   H V V   I R T S G

_ _ _ _ _ _ _
G S I L F T S

_ _ _ _!
G S V N

Q: How do you make a fruit punch?

A: _ _ _ _   _ _   _ _ _ _ _ _
T R E V   R G   Y L C R M T

_ _ _ _ _ _ _.
O V H H L M H

Q: Why did the Oreo go to the dentist?

A: _ _ _ _ _ _ _   _ _
Y V X Z F H V   R G

_ _ _ _   _ _ _
O L H G   R G H

_ _ _ _ _ _ _.
U R O O R M T

TEACHER FEATURE

Show off your awesome artistic talent! Draw each teacher in a box below and come up with a nickname for each!

ZZZZ
MMPH!

GOSSIP GAME

What are Nate's teachers talking about now? Make it up! Then fill in the bubbles. Get creative!

CRUSH WORTHY

Maya and Chad are crushing big-time!

Draw your dream crush here!

FIRE DRILL!

Nate and his crew at P.S. 38 have a fire drill. Find all the words hidden in the puzzle and help them get out fast!

FIRE

EMERGENCY

GAS LEAK

LOUDSPEAKER

EVACUATE

EXIT

ALARM

DRILL

SMOKE

BELL

LINE

SPRINKLER

A	R	S	M	O	K	E	E	C	E	S
K	B	I	P	N	M	R	L	B	V	B
U	E	E	D	R	S	L	D	N	A	A
F	L	M	A	A	I	E	I	R	C	F
G	L	L	E	R	A	N	E	E	U	R
A	A	N	D	R	U	K	K	R	A	L
S	I	N	A	T	G	B	X	L	T	L
L	O	U	D	S	P	E	A	K	E	R
E	N	A	L	S	R	X	N	B	L	R
A	I	A	R	I	C	I	P	C	X	D
K	L	P	F	U	C	T	R	E	Y	K

CREATE-A-NATE

Re-create the many faces of Nate—

draw each in one of the boxes below!

IT'S A SECRET!

Find Edna Birkdale's old journal!

SCRIBBLE CITY

It's time to get away. Take me to Scribble City!

Draw a city made <u>ONLY</u> from scribbles!

WHAT'S THAT YOU SAY?

Guess what's happening in each scene and fill in the speech bubbles. Quick! Nate's counting on you!

SILLY IDEAS

Have you ever done something silly that got you into hot water? Nate sure has! He and Chad jumped on the library beanbags and got covered in Styrofoam pellets!

LIST YOUR TOP 20 SILLY IDEAS.

1.

2.

3. Dressing the dog like a squirrel

4.

5.

6.

7. A mud bath—way too smelly!

8.

9.

10.

11.

12.

13. Leaving an egg salad sandwich in my locker

14.

15.

16.

17.

18.

19.

20.

BLACKTOP BRIGADE

What games make your recess seriously fun? See if you can solve these crossword puzzle clues and uncover all the games played at P.S. 38!

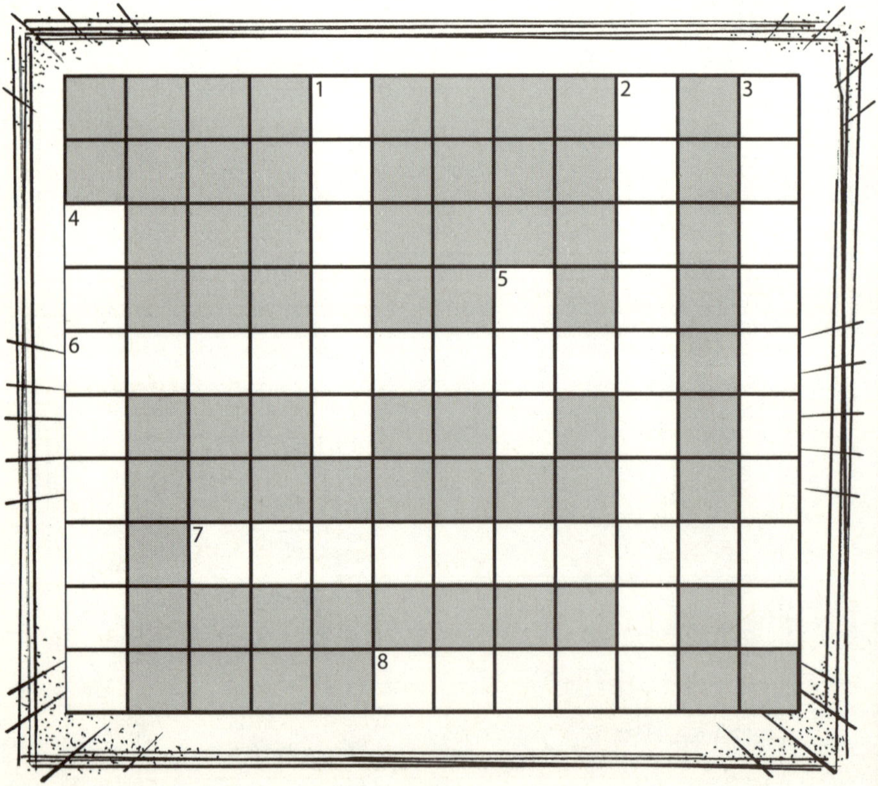

CLUES

ACROSS

6. Rhymes with "funky cars."

7. Round and round it goes. Rhymes with "feather hall."

8. Head down this, not up. Rhymes with "glide."

DOWN

1. Use your feet and no hands!

2. Not three but ______. Not round but ______.

3. Don't get hit! Rhymes with "lodge mall."

4. This rope's not for tug-o'-war.

5. You're it!

FUTURE FORECAST

Nate's not looking so hot! What happens next? You decide!

I'm sure Timmy will grow out of his bed-wetting phase! NATE did!

GESUNDHEIT!
THWAK!

... your TEST SCORE!
Dramatic Music!
A 43?

RECESS ROUNDUP

Recess is on, and the regular groups have gathered! Draw a line matching each group with Nate's label for them!

LOVEBIRDS

GOSSIP GIRLS

GET-A-LIFERS

GINA

SLACKERS

SHOW-OFFS

DOODLE DREAMS

Doodle your latest dream here!

Stretch your imagination and go wild!

OPERATION STATION

Set Dr. Cesspool straight. His operation has gone seriously wrong—fill in the speech bubbles and make things right!

SCRIBBLE SCENE

Scribbling is the name of the game! Finish this scribble and turn it into something FUN!

ACCIDENT-PRONE

Watch out! A ceiling tile just hit Nate on the head. Draw the wackiest accidents you can think of!

I'M LUCKY TO BE ALIVE!
THERE'S A TEENY TINY BUMP HERE.

EMOTION COMMOTION

Check out Principal Nichols's many emotions!

NOW DRAW THESE SAME THREE STAGES OF EMOTIONS FOR THE FOLLOWING CHARACTERS.

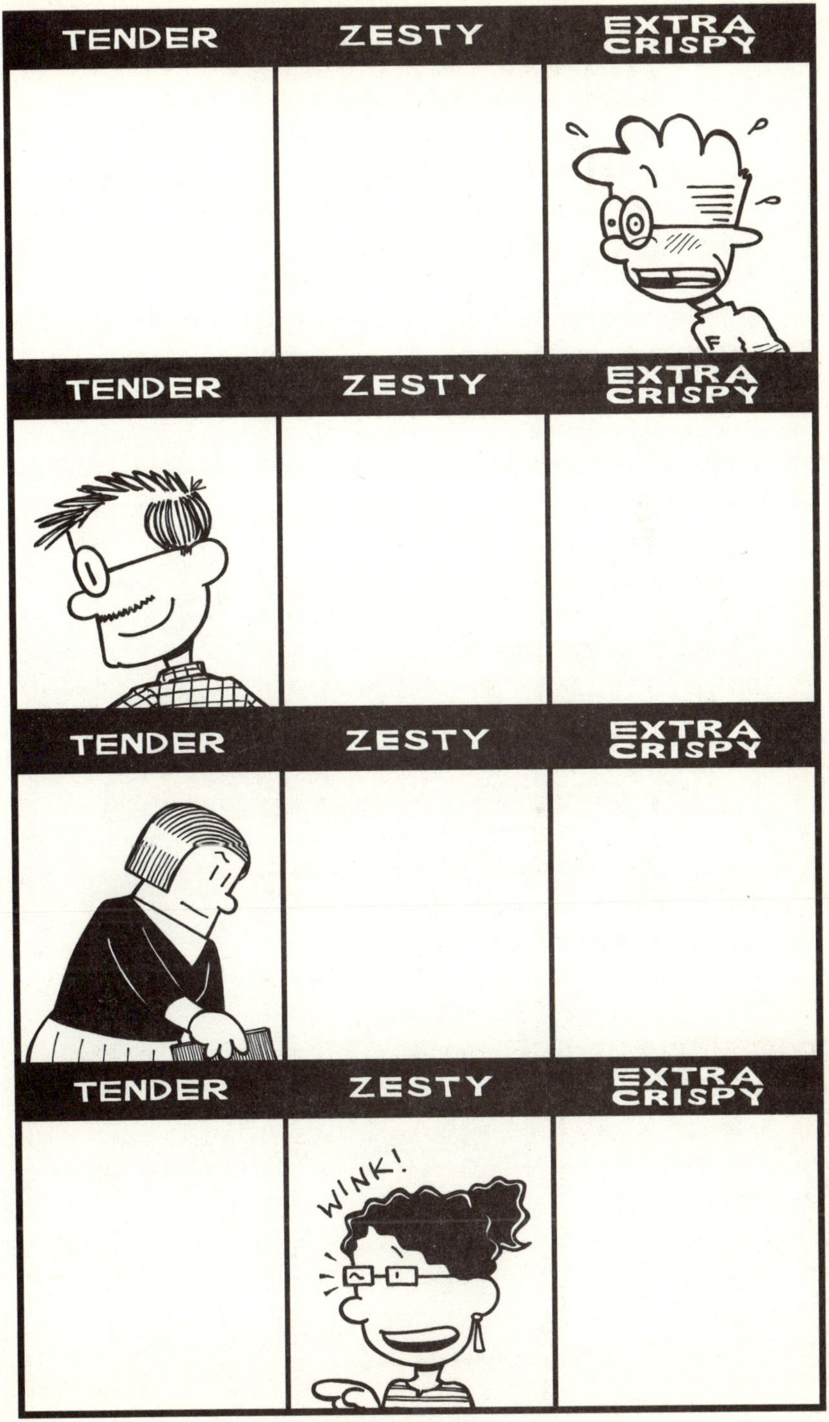
TENDER
ZESTY
EXTRA CRISPY
TENDER
ZESTY
EXTRA CRISPY
TENDER
ZESTY
EXTRA CRISPY
TENDER
ZESTY
EXTRA CRISPY
WINK!

DETENTION INVENTION

Uh-oh! What has Nate done now? He's in serious trouble. Decide why Nate's gotten detention and fill in the pink slips!

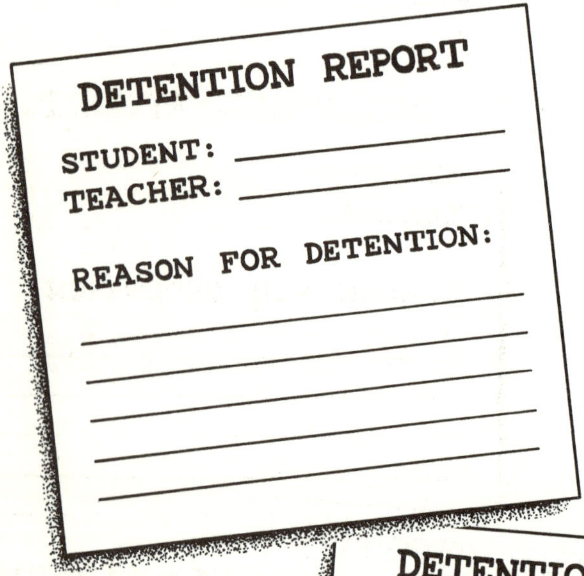

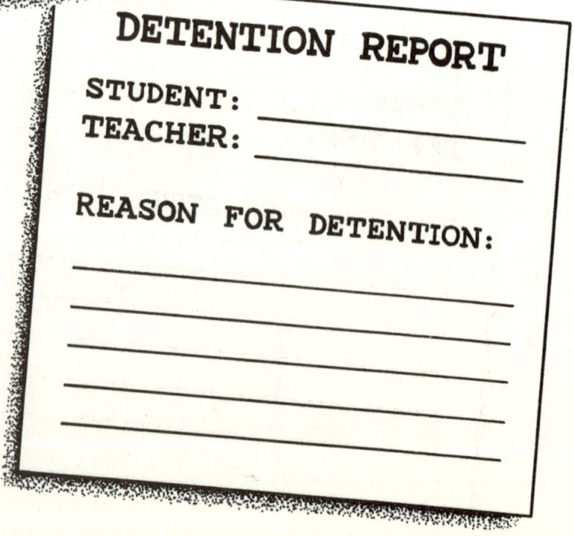

DETENTION REPORT
STUDENT:
TEACHER:
REASON FOR DETENTION:
DETENTION REPORT
STUDENT:
TEACHER:
REASON FOR DETENTION:
DETENTION REPORT
STUDENT:
TEACHER:
REASON FOR DETENTION:

COMIX-O-RAMA!

What happens when you combine one very angry Mrs. Godfrey; the new kid, Breckenridge; and dramatic Dee Dee? Draw it!

+

+

=

?

YOUR TITLE HERE

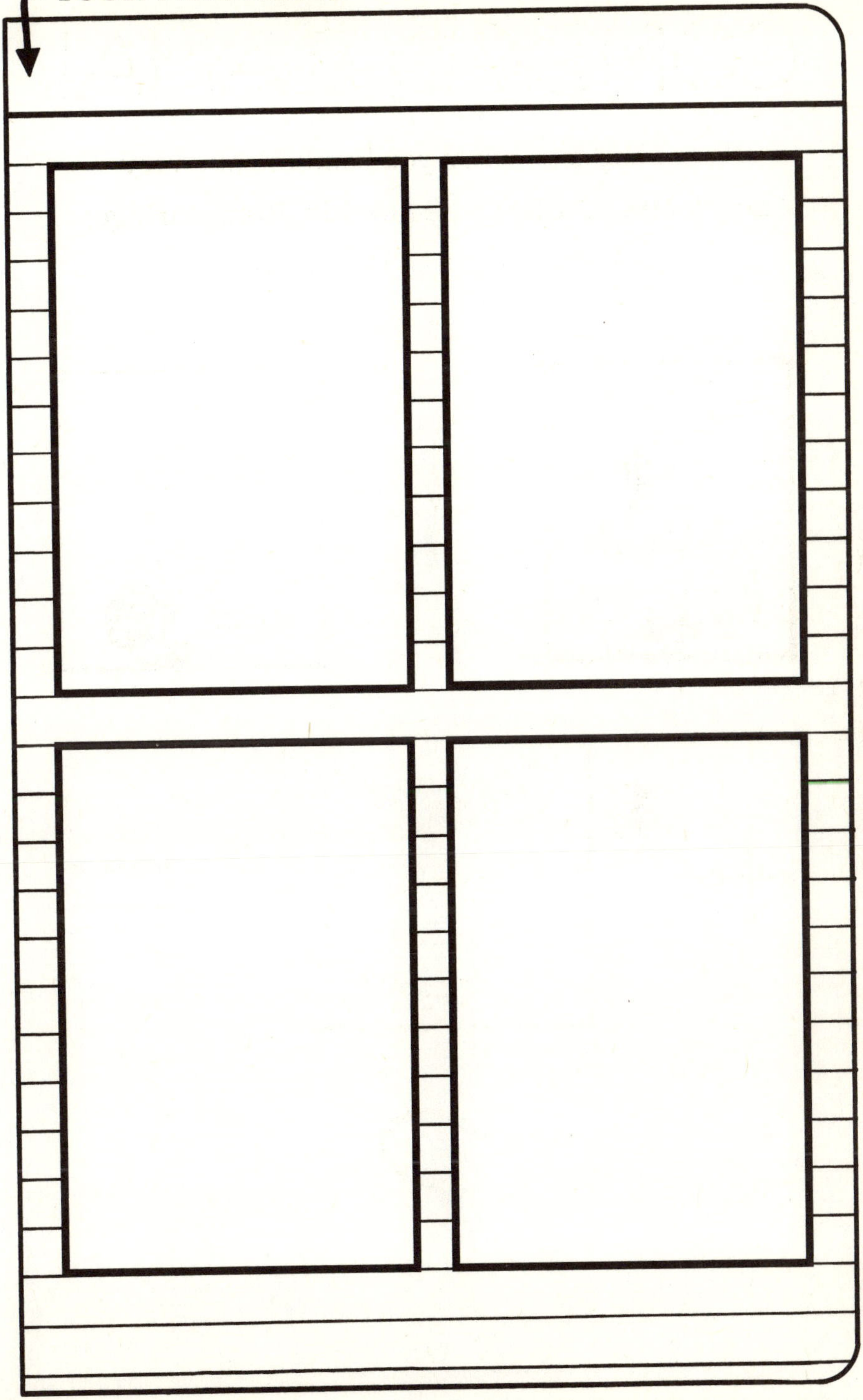

DOODLE DARE!

Nate dares you to FILL this page with doodles until there's NO white space left!

I'VE GOT A SUGGESTION!

Can Nate beat Gina's team to Principal Nichols?

PETAL POWER

The new kid, Breckenridge, created these drawings in art class, and Nate's jealous! Can you compete? Draw each flower in a box below!

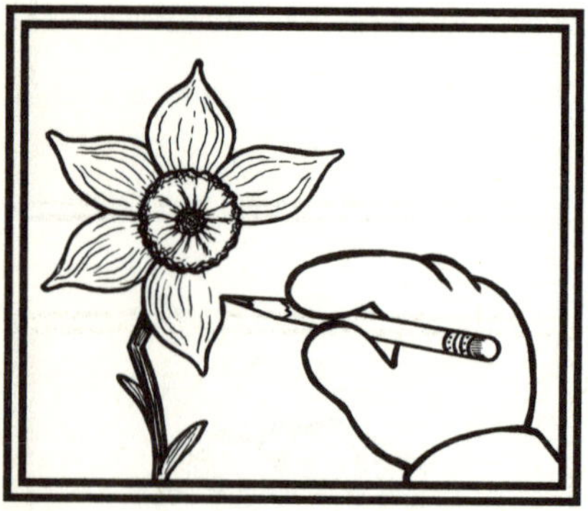

MUST-HAVE MAYHEM

One hundred years ago, P.S. 38 sure was different! There was no library (which Gina can't live without!) and no lunchroom (a must-have for Chad!).

LIST YOUR TOP 20 MUST-HAVES HERE!

1.

2.

3.

4. my favorite book

5.

6.

7.

8. my pet named ____________________

9.

10.
11.
12.
13.
14.
15. ice cream
16.
17.
18.
19.
20.

FLASHBACK!

What happened before each of these disasters?

You be the judge! Draw it!

SPLOOSH!

MS. CLARKE! WHAT HAPPENED?
A CEILING TILE FELL ON NATE!

HA HA HA HA HA
HA HA HA HA HA
CAUTION!

MR. ROSA'S ROOM

Let your inner artist out and head to Mr. Rosa's! Find all the art supplies in the word scramble on the opposite page, and your art goes on the wall first!

GLUE

PASTELS

TAPE

CLAY

COLOR WHEEL

DRAWING PAPER

SCISSORS

PENCIL

BRUSHES

EASEL

STICKERS

PAINT

E	L	A	I	E	E	C	Y	A	T	O	E
E	C	R	H	T	E	S	R	R	U	R	S
S	O	R	S	O	W	S	D	L	N	L	S
C	L	A	Y	L	T	D	T	E	E	S	L
I	O	R	E	I	N	A	H	T	P	N	O
S	R	E	K	C	I	T	S	A	A	E	R
S	W	A	G	N	A	A	E	P	T	A	P
O	H	S	E	E	P	W	L	N	E	W	S
R	E	P	A	P	G	N	I	W	A	R	D
S	E	H	S	U	R	B	E	C	I	T	E
G	L	U	E	S	U	S	I	E	S	S	R
D	L	A	L	I	E	S	S	L	E	L	P

BUDDY UP

Principal Nichols asks Nate to be a buddy to the new kid at P.S. 38. How well do you know him?

1. His last name is . . .
   - a. Carter-Huffington
   - b. Puffington
   - c. Worthington
   - d. Ortiz

2. His old nickname was . . .
   - a. Bobby
   - b. Joey
   - c. Johnny
   - d. Fred

3. When he grows up he wants to be a . . .

a. pianist

b. basketball player

c. botanist

d. biologist

4. He's really good at drawing . . .

a. frogs

b. flowers

c. waterfalls

d. donuts

EXTRA CREDIT

Write out his full name:

____

HEADLINE TIME!

These are some <u>CRAZY</u> situations. . . . Come up with a headline for each scene!

Then you mix the colors together, and-
LOOK OUT!

It's so... plush.
Are those mushrooms edible?
SQUISH
SQUISH

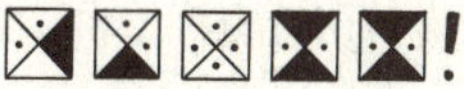

FRIEND ZONE

Draw lines from column A to column B and choose a hilarious pair you'd love to see as BEST friends!

Column A

Column B

GINA VS. NATE

When Gina says one thing, Nate always says the opposite! Fill in Nate's speech bubbles below.

DOODLE DRAMA!

Give Dee Dee something to shout about!

Fill the page with dynamic doodles!!

DOUBLE TROUBLE

It looks like each of these pairs is in trouble—help them out and fill in the bubbles!

MY NEW BFF

Check out Nate and his new friend, Breckenridge. Are they really riding off into the sunset together. . . ? No way!

DRAW A PORTRAIT OF YOURSELF AND A NEW FRIEND YOU'VE JUST MADE!

DOODLE IN THE DARK

Now for something totally different! Close your eyes, then draw your coolest Halloween costume. Open your eyes and see how it turned out!

SUPERHERO STRONG

Ultra-Nate and his fearless friends must unite to save the planet. Fill in the grid so that each superhero shows up once in every row, column, and box!

T = **TEDDY TITAN**

M = **MEGA-CHAD**

C = **CAPTAIN FRANTASTIC**

B = **BUDDY BOY**

MEGA-CHAD! TEDDY TITAN! CAPTAIN FRANTASTIC! LET'S GO!
HOLD IT!

	M		
C	B	M	
			B
B		C	

We have a NEW crime fighter I'd like you to work with!
Who?

They call me... BUDDY BOY!

TIME MACHINE

Image you're Edna Birkdale, and you went to P.S. 38 one hundred years ago! Draw a comic about your blast to the past!

The names back then sure sounded different!

LIST YOUR TOP 20 NAMES FROM 100 YEARS AGO. (*MAKE THEM UP!)

1.	11.
2.	12.
3.	13.
4.	14. Abraham
5. Penelope	15.
6.	16.
7.	17.
8.	18. Thaddeus
9.	19.
10.	20.

WE ARE THE CHAMPIONS!

Can Nate and his friends win the scavenger hunt?

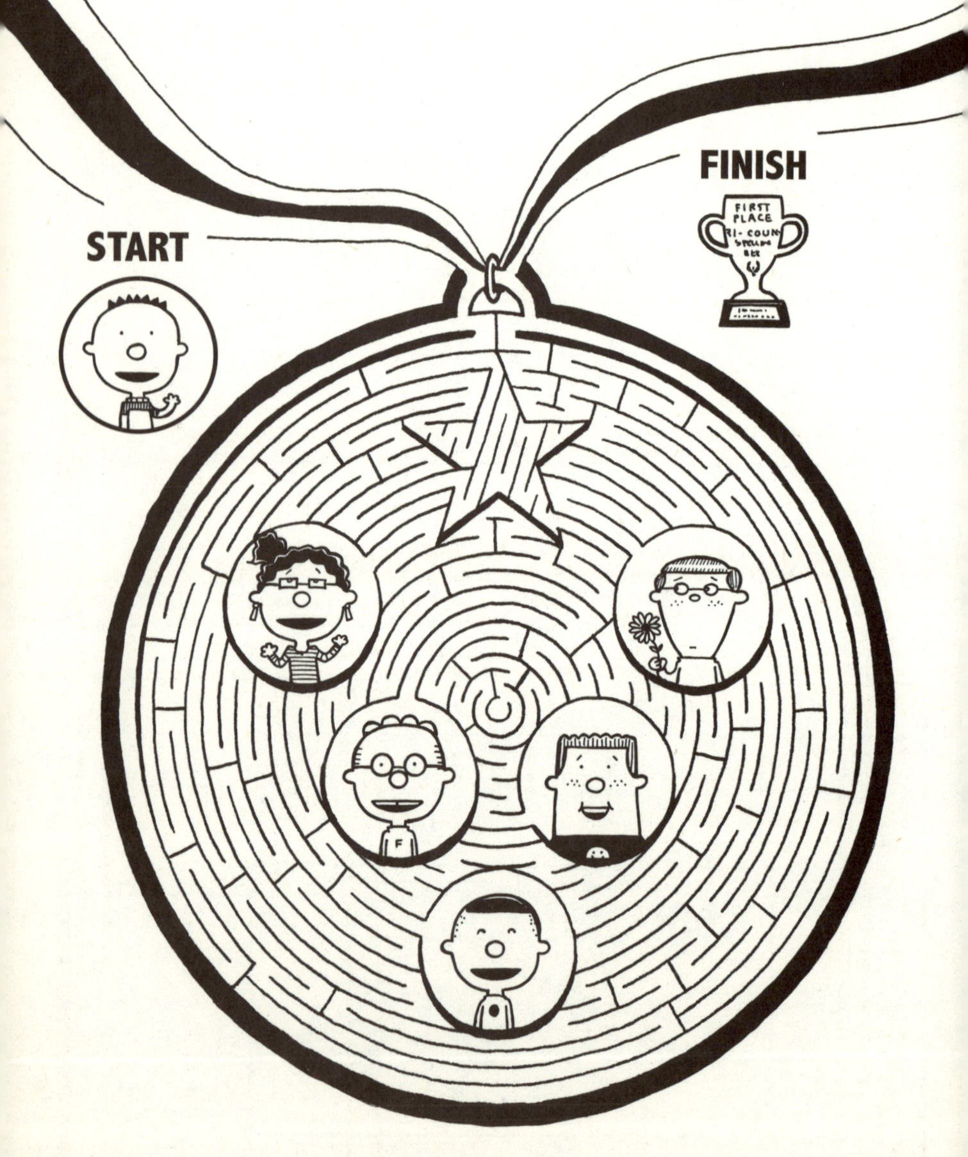

GRAFFITI GAME

Oh no! Breckenridge is accused of covering his desk with drawings and graffiti! Go wild and fill <u>this</u> desk with graffiti, too.

SWAMPCAT STORY

Mega-Chad's up against some serious danger! Quick, finish the comic and save him from disaster!

You were AMAZING!
Hold it. Some-thing's wrong.

MASTER TALENT

Francis is the master of trivia, Dee Dee does drama, Nate's a comics genius, Teddy tells jokes, and Chad is king of cuisine!

LIST YOUR TOP 15 MASTER TALENTS!

1.
2.
3.
4.
5.

6.
7.
8.
9.
10.
11.

12.
13.
14.
15.

NOW DRAW YOURSELF DOING THE THING YOU'RE BEST AT (AKA YOUR #1 MASTER TALENT).

FORTUNE-TELLER

Look into your crystal ball! Now predict the future for each of these characters. . . .

NATE:

CHAD:

TEDDY:

FRANCIS:

DEE DEE:

ARTUR:

FESTIVE FASHIONS

Dee Dee loves dressing up for holidays and makes sure her outfits are seriously festive! Draw what Dee Dee would wear on each of the following holidays!

THANKSGIVING

HALLOWEEN

ST. PATRICK'S DAY

JULY 4th

VALENTINE'S DAY

SCAVENGER HUNT

Ready, set, write! List everything you see in this cool school poster! Circle each item once you've added it to your list.

1.
2.
3.
4.
5.
6.
7.
8.
9.
10.

TROUBLE BUBBLE

What words do you NEVER want to hear from a teacher? Fill in the bubbles below!

ANSWER KEY

FIELD DAY FOLLIES (p. 5)

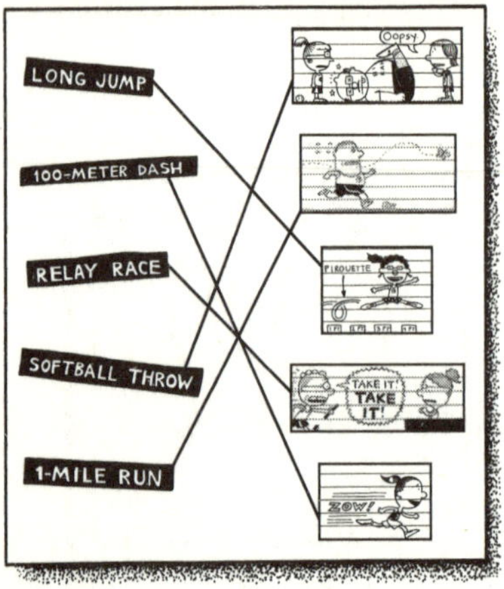

FIELD DAY FOLLIES (pp. 6–7)

W	B	G	E	A	L	S	W	G	O	S	O	I	O	E	B
O	O	A	G	C	R	T	H	R	C	T	D	C	C	L	E
R	N	E	O	E	T	H	H	H	Y	R	T	A	E	T	O
H	C	C	C	R	P	R	S	E	A	W	R	E	A	U	O
T	A	A	O	F	O	E	T	L	G	I	R	S	E	G	T
E	S	R	U	O	C	E	L	C	A	T	S	B	O	O	E
E	E	K	O	R	W	L	C	W	G	O	E	R	H	F	I
B	U	C	R	A	E	E	H	A	T	E	H	C	O	W	O
S	H	A	H	R	R	G	B	G	D	T	A	A	S	A	E
I	E	S	S	U	G	G	G	G	C	G	B	P	R	R	E
R	E	O	C	W	R	E	L	A	Y	S	R	A	W	A	E
F	R	T	T	L	E	D	O	E	T	C	S	S	R	S	A
E	C	A	R	W	O	R	R	A	B	L	E	E	H	W	B
W	A	T	E	R	B	A	L	L	O	O	N	T	O	S	S
A	G	O	O	R	O	C	L	R	I	E	E	R	T	S	O
R	W	P	C	E	W	E	S	R	E	T	A	L	R	T	S

BREAKFAST BONANZA (pp. 16–17)

A	I	D	P	C	M	T	T	G	F	T	I	R	C	F	E	E
S	C	F	O	C	A	F	W	A	E	R	G	S	A	A	F	O
H	C	I	W	D	N	A	S	T	S	A	F	K	A	E	R	B
T	G	R	O	D	O	A	A	N	F	T	R	E	M	R	O	A
K	E	B	A	O	C	A	U	O	W	P	E	E	A	T	S	R
O	O	C	H	M	A	R	S	S	R	O	O	G	T	R	T	N
C	T	F	U	W	B	P	A	I	C	P	R	N	C	S	E	N
P	R	S	F	H	C	L	G	R	O	A	A	B	G	P	D	G
E	A	S	N	A	O	R	E	S	F	G	C	E	H	O	F	E
D	U	T	A	C	B	P	E	D	F	E	D	G	N	S	L	L
O	T	S	A	S	G	R	A	P	E	F	R	U	I	T	A	F
R	A	L	M	U	F	F	I	N	E	G	T	R	R	M	K	H
W	H	D	O	H	M	L	A	H	C	S	G	C	W	G	E	O
L	A	B	A	E	T	E	E	W	A	A	T	S	T	A	S	B
S	S	E	K	E	T	S	N	O	K	E	K	R	L	B	O	E
O	A	A	U	W	S	A	T	R	E	L	A	E	M	T	A	O
E	L	M	E	H	F	P	E	E	T	L	F	O	S	M	E	C

READY? SET. POP QUIZ! (pp. 18–19)

1. True
2. True
3. False
4. False
5. True
6. True
7. True
8. False

MUSIC MAN (p. 20)

Drum
Guitar
Trombone
Oboe
Flute
Bass
Semaphore: You're jammin'!

PLAY ALONG! (p. 21)

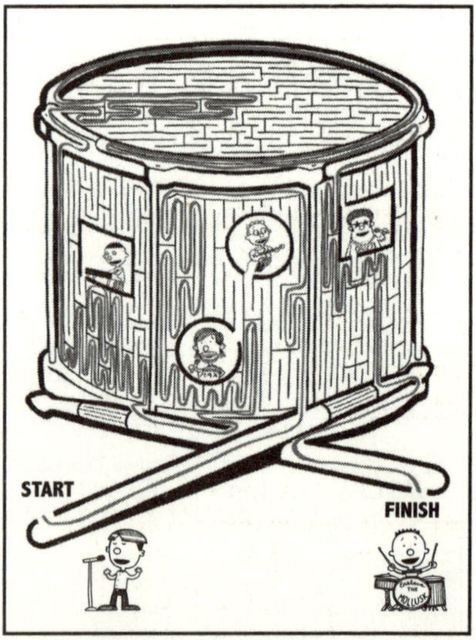

KNOCK, KNOCK! (pp. 22–23)

Is there an owl in here?
Leaf me alone.
Lettuce in and you'll find out.

COPY THAT! (pp. 30–31)

Semaphore: You're an artist!

MIDDLE SCHOOL MASH-UP (p. 32)

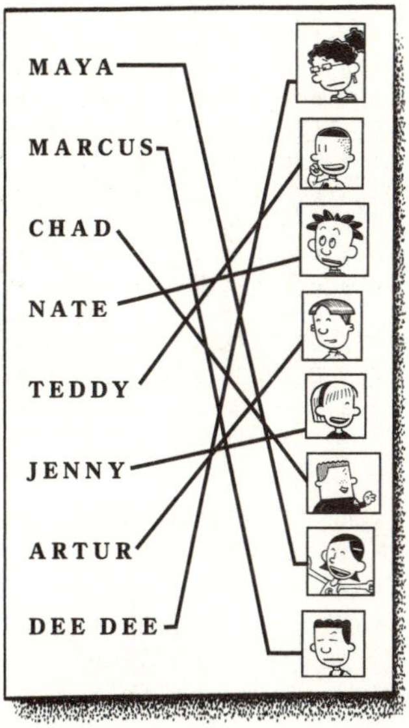

LUCKY LOCKER (pp. 40–41)

Semaphore: Amazing!

MESSY MAZE! (p. 42)

FITNESS ZONE (pp. 46–47)

B	V	A	E	K	R	T	A	I	S	O	A
K	O	G	S	A	A	R	S	B	O	L	K
C	L	L	A	B	T	E	K	S	A	B	I
A	L	A	W	N	V	S	O	C	M	I	S
R	E	C	C	O	S	F	R	I	A	A	A
T	Y	O	R	O	T	O	Y	T	E	Y	I
R	B	L	B	B	S	K	N	S	R	B	L
C	A	I	A	S	L	C	E	A	O	L	I
I	L	L	E	S	C	Y	I	N	B	O	N
C	L	C	Y	S	W	I	M	M	I	N	G
C	R	B	H	O	C	K	E	Y	C	S	S
W	R	E	S	T	L	I	N	G	S	S	T

CAPTION ATTRACTION (pp. 54–55)

Semaphores: Yuck!
Eww!

P.S. 38'S "LEAST LIKELY TO GET DETENTION" CLUB! (p. 56)

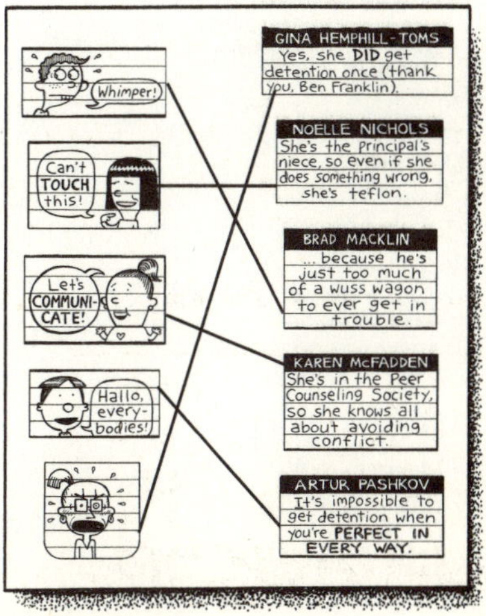

ROLL CALL (pp. 62–63)

										1 M			
					2 A		3 M	A	Y	A			
					R					R			
					T			4 P		C			
					U			I		U			
				5 F	R	A	N	C	I	S			
								K					
				6 J				L			7 S		
			8 D	E	E	D	E	E			P		9 N
	10 C			N				S		11 G	I	N	A
	H			N							T		T
12 R	A	N	D	Y							S		E
	D						13 T	E	D	D	Y		

FLOWER POWER (p. 71)

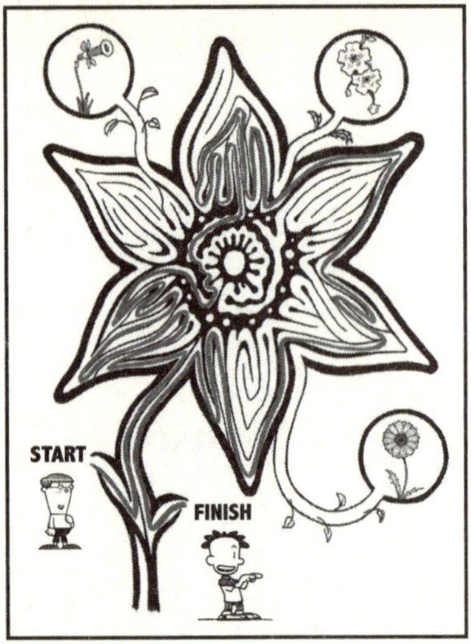

SMARTY-PANTS (pp. 74–75)

1. False
2. False
3. False
4. True
5. False
6. False
7. True
8. False
9. True
10. True

Bonus: False

HOCKEY TALK (pp. 76–77)

C	E	F	A	C	E	O	F	F	L	E	L	B	I
L	D	D	C	N	C	T	A	L	K	I	L	K	I
L	R	B	E	A	I	C	E	I	E	R	F	C	A
D	I	N	L	D	T	F	R	S	B	R	I	I	K
E	L	D	R	I	C	R	E	A	S	E	R	T	S
F	L	W	S	E	A	E	D	Y	I	L	L	S	L
E	E	R	P	I	R	P	L	I	O	R	A	N	A
N	C	O	N	N	P	P	I	R	W	P	L	C	D
S	A	L	B	L	L	Y	G	N	A	P	D	R	A
E	S	Z	A	L	E	R	H	R	B	U	O	L	L
N	F	Y	M	O	I	O	T	W	L	C	I	R	D
L	E	L	L	S	G	R	L	E	D	K	O	L	N
R	P	E	N	A	L	T	Y	S	H	O	T	S	B
L	C	C	R	O	B	L	A	E	L	I	R	C	S

MARCUS MADNESS (pp. 80–81)
Semaphore: Go, Nate!

GOOD GODFREY! (pp. 82–83)

1. (b) Godzilla
2. (d) Social studies
3. (c) Gina
4. (b) Neat notes
5. (c) Dance the macarena

STORY SWAP (p. 101)

NEW-KID NO-NO'S (pp. 104–105)
Semaphore: Eww!

CARRIED AWAY! (pp. 106–107)
Semaphore: Don't hold back!

THE SKY'S THE LIMIT (p. 108)

TOUCHDOWN! (pp. 110–111)

K	H	T	O	U	C	H	D	O	W	N
U	C	M	N	E	L	K	C	A	T	P
L	M	A	M	B	B	C	M	P	H	L
A	Y	K	B	B	Z	O	L	W	C	A
O	D	I	C	R	D	L	R	C	X	Y
G	N	E	P	I	E	B	C	B	U	S
D	T	K	F	A	K	T	U	L	P	M
L	G	S	E	E	S	Z	R	C	C	K
E	C	X	F	J	N	S	B	A	X	C
I	B	S	M	G	J	S	J	W	U	Z
F	G	D	R	Y	A	M	E	J	U	Q

BANDMATES
(pp. 114–115)

A	T	N	F
N	F	A	T
T	N	F	A
F	A	T	N

LONG, LONG AGO (pp. 120–124)
Semaphore: Look out, Nate!

NURSE'S OFFICE (pp. 130–131)

E	R	H	P	O	P	I	L	L	O	L	E	E
C	T	S	P	N	V	O	C	U	C	S	T	O
S	E	I	P	P	O	F	N	T	C	U	S	R
S	T	A	O	R	H	T	E	R	O	S	E	O
T	O	E	H	E	O	R	U	V	G	O	H	B
S	O	B	T	T	D	D	C	P	E	U	E	A
C	O	U	G	H	S	Y	R	U	P	R	N	N
R	E	T	E	M	O	M	R	E	H	T	I	D
A	U	V	L	U	O	S	N	E	T	O	C	A
P	D	S	E	H	S	H	C	M	O	O	I	G
E	E	E	C	L	I	P	B	O	A	R	D	E
C	A	I	O	T	R	N	E	E	P	S	E	A
T	H	R	U	N	N	Y	N	O	S	E	M	A

CAPTION REACTION
(pp. 134–135)
Semaphores: Yuck!
Yikes!
Ouch!

LAUGH ATTACK
(pp. 142–143)
Because you can see right through them!
Give it boxing lessons.
Because it lost its filling.

FIRE DRILL! (pp. 148–149)

A	R	S	M	O	K	E	E	C	E	S
K	B	I	P	N	M	R	L	B	V	B
U	E	E	D	R	S	L	D	N	A	A
F	L	M	A	A	I	E	I	R	C	F
G	L	L	E	R	A	N	E	E	U	R
A	A	N	D	R	U	K	K	R	A	L
S	I	N	A	T	G	B	X	L	T	L
L	O	U	D	S	P	E	A	K	E	R
E	N	A	L	S	R	X	N	B	L	R
A	I	A	R	I	C	I	P	C	X	D
K	L	P	F	U	C	T	R	E	Y	K

IT'S A SECRET! (p. 152)

BLACKTOP BRIGADE (pp. 158–159)

				[1]S					[2]F		[3]D
				O					O		O
[4]J				C					U		D
U				C			[5]T		R		G
[6]M	O	N	K	E	Y	B	A	R	S		E
P				R			G		Q		B
R									U		A
O		[7]T	E	T	H	E	R	B	A	L	L
P									R		L
E					[8]S	L	I	D	E		

RECESS ROUNDUP (p. 162)

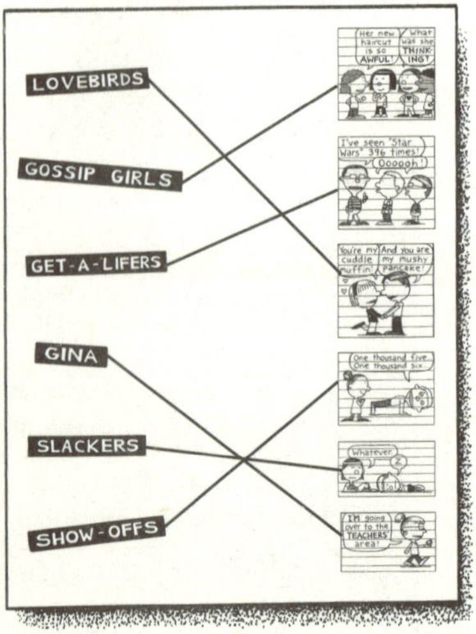

ACCIDENT-PRONE (pp. 166–167)

Semaphores: Oh no!
Bananas!
That's crazy!

I'VE GOT A SUGGESTION! (p. 175)

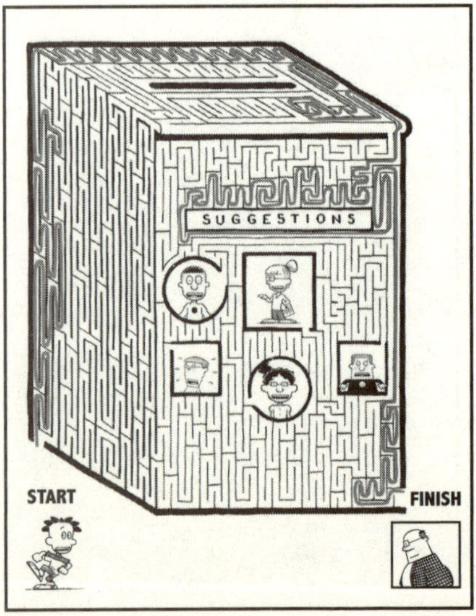

MUST-HAVE MAYHEM (pp. 178–179)

Semaphore: No doubt!

FLASHBACK! (pp. 180–181)

Semaphore: Whoa!

MR. ROSA'S ROOM (pp. 182–183)

E	L	A	I	E	E	C	Y	A	T	O	E
E	C	R	H	T	E	S	R	R	U	R	S
S	O	R	S	O	W	S	D	L	N	L	S
C	L	A	Y	L	T	D	T	E	E	S	L
I	O	R	E	I	N	A	H	T	P	N	O
S	R	E	K	C	I	T	S	A	A	E	R
S	W	A	G	N	A	A	E	P	T	A	P
O	H	S	E	E	P	W	L	N	E	W	S
R	E	P	A	P	G	N	I	W	A	R	D
S	E	H	S	U	R	B	E	C	I	T	E
G	L	U	E	S	U	S	I	E	S	S	R
D	L	A	L	I	E	S	S	L	E	L	P

BUDDY UP
(pp. 184–185)
1. (b) Puffington
2. (a) Bobby
3. (c) botanist
4. (b) flowers
Extra credit:
Breckenridge Puffington III

HEADLINE TIME!
(pp. 186–187)
Semaphores:
Danger!
Gross!

SUPERHERO STRONG
(pp. 194–195)

T	M	B	C
C	B	M	T
M	C	T	B
B	T	C	M

WE ARE THE CHAMPIONS! (p. 198)

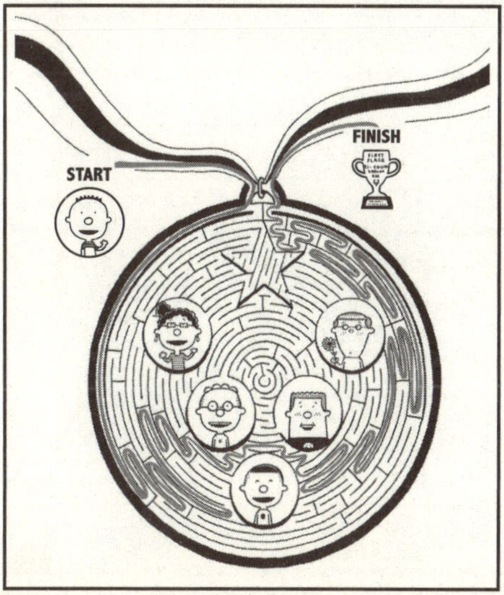

SWAMPCAT STORY
(pp. 200–201)
Semaphore: Comix to the rescue!

SCAVENGER HUNT
(p. 208)
school
cane
glasses
turtle
clouds
birds
butterfly
balloons
party hat
Bobcat

BLASTIN' OFF!

Our school newspaper, "The Weekly Bugle," was struggling.

Good question, Chad. Bottom line: The newspaper was totally lame and needed a major makeover. Luckily, I knew just the person for the job.

My gossip column, ***BUGLE BLASTS***, was a hit with everyone – except P.S. 38's #1 jerk, Randy Betancourt.

PRINCIPAL SENDS NATE TO DETENTION...AGAIN! That was going to be the headline, right? Wrong.

There was so much going on at school, I completely missed the biggest news flash of all—at **HOME**.

Very important...
and very **BAD**!

Find out!
Read ***BIG NATE BLASTS OFF***!

READ ALL THE BIG NATE BOOKS TODAY!

To learn about the activity books, comic compilations, and more visit **www.bignatebooks.com**.

HARPER

An Imprint of HarperCollins*Publishers*